SHADOWS OF TRUST

A Romantic Thriller

By Jasmine Deatherage

I0679198

Table of Contents

Chapter 1: Perfect Facades

The morning sun cast long shadows across the hardwood floors of the Sterling home, creating patterns that danced with the gentle sway of the oak trees outside. Victoria Sterling stood at the kitchen island, her manicured fingers wrapped around a ceramic mug that read "World's Best Realtor" – a gift from Marcus on their third anniversary. The coffee was still steaming, but her attention was fixed on the tablet displaying her schedule for the day.

"Three showings, two closings, and a client dinner," she murmured to herself, scrolling through the appointments with practiced efficiency. At thirty-two, Tori had built a reputation as one of the most successful real estate agents in the greater Seattle area. Her specialty was luxury properties, the kind of homes that graced the covers of architectural magazines and commanded prices that made even wealthy clients pause.

"Talking to yourself again?" Marcus's voice carried a hint of amusement as he descended the stairs, adjusting his tie with the same precision he applied to everything in his life. At thirty-five, he possessed the kind of understated confidence that drew people to him without effort. His dark hair was perfectly styled, and his gray eyes held a warmth that had first captured Tori's attention five years ago at a charity auction.

"Just organizing my thoughts," she replied, turning to face her husband with a smile that still made her heart skip after all these years. "Big day ahead. The Whitmore property is finally getting some serious interest."

Marcus moved behind her, his hands settling on her shoulders as he pressed a gentle kiss to the top of her head. "The one up on Mercer Island? The glass house with the infinity pool?"

"That's the one. Twelve million dollars of architectural perfection, and I think I've found the perfect buyer." Tori leaned back against his chest, savoring the moment of quiet intimacy before their day pulled them in different directions. "Elena Vasquez.
She's new to the area, relocating from New York for business. Has the financial backing and seems

genuinely interested in the unique features."

"Sounds promising." Marcus's hands moved to massage the slight tension in her shoulders, a gesture so familiar it had become their morning ritual. "What kind of business?"

"Import-export, I think she said. Something international." Tori set down her mug and turned in his arms, straightening his already perfect tie. "She has excellent taste and doesn't seem fazed by the price point. I have a good feeling about this one."

Marcus studied her face, noting the excitement that always lit up her features when she talked about a potential sale. It was one of the things he loved most about her – the genuine passion she brought to her work, the way she could see the perfect match between a property and its future owner. "Just be careful showing that place. It's pretty isolated."

"I always am." She stood on her tiptoes to kiss him, a brief but tender connection that spoke of years of shared mornings and mutual trust. "Besides, what could possibly go wrong? It's broad daylight, and Elena seems lovely. Very professional, well-dressed, asked all the right questions during our phone consultation."

Marcus nodded, though something flickered in his eyes – a shadow so brief that Tori might have imagined it. In his line of work as a real estate developer, he'd learned to trust his instincts about people and situations. But he also knew that Tori was capable and experienced. She'd been showing properties for eight years, and her safety record was impeccable.

"What about you?" Tori asked, smoothing down his lapels. "Big day at Sterling Development?"

"The usual. Meeting with architects about the downtown project, reviewing construction timelines, dealing with city permits." Marcus's company had grown significantly over the past few years, specializing in mixed-use developments that revitalized urban areas while maintaining their character. It was work he found fulfilling, a far cry from his previous life that Tori knew nothing about.

"The sustainable housing initiative?"

"Among other things. We're hoping to break ground next month if all the approvals come through." He glanced at his watch, a sleek piece that had been a wedding gift
from Tori. "I should head out. Conference call with the investors starts in an hour."

They moved through their morning routine with the synchronized efficiency of a couple who had learned each other's rhythms. Marcus gathered his briefcase and jacket while Tori collected her showing materials – property brochures, contracts, her tablet loaded with comparable sales data. The Whitmore house was a significant listing, and she wanted to be prepared for any questions or negotiations.

"Dinner tonight?" Marcus asked as they walked toward the garage together.

"If the showing goes well, definitely. If not, I might be working late on follow-up calls and paperwork." Tori's BMW was parked next to Marcus's Range Rover, both vehicles reflecting their owners' success and attention to detail.

"Either way, I'll pick up something from that Italian place you like. We can celebrate or commiserate as needed." Marcus opened her car door for her, another small courtesy that had never faded from their relationship.

"You're too good to me," she said, settling into the driver's seat and starting the engine.

"Not possible." He leaned down to kiss her once

more, his hand briefly cupping her cheek. "I love you, Tori. Have a great day."

"Love you too."

As they backed out of their driveway, Marcus watched Tori's car disappear around the corner before heading in the opposite direction toward downtown Seattle. The morning traffic was building, but he barely noticed the familiar congestion. His mind was elsewhere, caught on something he couldn't quite identify. It wasn't unusual for him to feel protective of Tori – she was the most important thing in his world, the anchor that had given his life meaning after years of drifting.

But today felt different somehow. Maybe it was the isolation of the Whitmore property, or perhaps it was the way Tori had mentioned her new client. Elena Vasquez. The name didn't ring any bells, but Marcus had learned long ago that danger often came from the most unexpected sources.

He shook off the feeling as he merged onto Interstate 5. Tori was right – what could possibly go wrong during a routine property showing? She was meeting a legitimate client at a legitimate listing during daylight hours. His protective instincts were
probably just overactive, a remnant from a time when

vigilance had been a matter of survival.

Still, as he navigated through the morning traffic toward his office, Marcus couldn't shake the sense that something was about to change. It was a feeling he'd learned to trust during his previous career, though he'd hoped never to experience it again. The life he'd built with Tori was supposed to be safe, predictable, normal. It was everything he'd wanted after years of living in shadows.

But shadows, Marcus knew better than most, had a way of following you no matter how far you ran.

Meanwhile, across the city, Tori was reviewing her notes about the Whitmore property as she drove toward Mercer Island. The house was a masterpiece of modern architecture, all clean lines and floor-to-ceiling windows that maximized the stunning views of Lake Washington. It had been on the market for six months, which wasn't unusual for a property in that price range, but Tori sensed that Elena Vasquez might be the buyer they'd been waiting for.

The client had been thorough in her questions during their initial phone consultation, asking about everything from the home's smart technology systems to the landscaping maintenance requirements. She'd seemed particularly interested in the property's privacy features – the gated entrance, the extensive grounds that provided natural barriers from neighboring homes, the state-of-the-art security system.

"Perfect for someone who values discretion," Elena had said, her slight accent adding an exotic quality to her voice. "I do a lot of work from home and need a space where I can conduct business without interruption."

Tori had understood completely. Many of her high-end clients were executives or entrepreneurs who needed homes that could function as private retreats and professional spaces. The Whitmore house was ideal for that purpose, with a dedicated office wing and multiple entertaining areas that could accommodate both intimate gatherings and larger business functions.

As she crossed the bridge to Mercer Island, Tori felt the familiar thrill of anticipation that came with a promising showing. This was what she loved most about her job – not just the financial rewards, though they were certainly welcome, but the satisfaction of matching the right people with the right property. There was something almost
magical about that moment when a client walked into

a house and knew they were home.

The Whitmore property sat on three acres at the end of a private road, surrounded by mature evergreens that provided both beauty and seclusion. Tori had always admired the way the architect had designed the house to complement its natural setting, using materials like cedar and stone that seemed to grow from the landscape itself.

She pulled into the circular driveway and checked her watch. Elena was due to arrive in fifteen minutes, which gave Tori time to open up the house and do a final walk through to ensure everything was perfect. The current owners were traveling in Europe, so she had complete access to prepare the property for showing.

Using her lockbox key, Tori entered through the front door and immediately disabled the security system. The house always took her breath away, even after multiple visits. The entry foyer featured a dramatic staircase with a floating design that seemed to defy gravity, while the living areas beyond showcased the panoramic water views that made the property so special.

She moved through the rooms systematically, opening

blinds to let in the natural light, adjusting the temperature to a comfortable level, and checking that all the high-end appliances and technology systems were functioning properly. The house was immaculate, as always, but Tori had learned that attention to these details could make the difference between a showing and a sale.

As she finished her preparations, Tori heard the sound of a car approaching on the gravel driveway. Elena was precisely on time, which Tori appreciated in a client. Punctuality often indicated serious interest and respect for everyone's time.

Through the floor-to-ceiling windows, Tori watched a sleek black sedan pull up to the front entrance. The woman who emerged was exactly as Tori had imagined from their phone conversations – elegant, well-dressed, and carrying herself with the confidence of someone accustomed to success. Elena appeared to be in her late twenties, with dark hair pulled back in a sophisticated chignon and wearing a tailored suit that probably cost more than most people's monthly salary.

Tori opened the front door with her professional smile in place. "Elena? I'm Victoria Sterling. It's wonderful to meet you in person."

"The pleasure is mine," Elena replied, extending a manicured hand for a firm handshake. Her smile was warm, but her dark eyes seemed to take in every detail of both Tori and the property's entrance. "This is even more impressive than the photos suggested."

"Wait until you see the views from the main living area," Tori said, gesturing for her client to enter. "The architect really maximized the property's natural advantages."

As Elena stepped into the foyer, Tori noticed that she moved with an unusual grace, almost like a dancer or someone trained in martial arts. It was an odd observation, but Tori had learned to pick up on subtle details about her clients. Understanding their backgrounds and preferences helped her tailor her presentations more effectively.

"Shall we start with the main level and work our way up?" Tori suggested, leading Elena toward the living areas.

"Actually," Elena said, her voice taking on a slightly different tone, "I was hoping we could start with the more private areas. The office wing you mentioned, perhaps? I'm very interested in the security features and how well the space would work for confidential business meetings."

"Of course." Tori adjusted her planned route without hesitation. Flexibility was key in her business, and if Elena wanted to focus on the office areas, that suggested serious interest in using the property for business purposes. "The office wing is actually my favorite part of the house. It's completely separate from the main living areas, with its own entrance and parking area."

As they walked through the house, Elena asked thoughtful questions about everything from the internet infrastructure to the soundproofing between rooms. She seemed particularly interested in the sight lines from various windows and the response time for local emergency services.

"You're very thorough," Tori observed as they entered the office wing. "I can tell you're someone who thinks through all the details."

"In my line of work, details can be the difference between success and failure," Elena replied, running her hand along the custom millwork that lined the office walls. "This space is perfect. Very private, very secure."

"The current owners had it designed for exactly that purpose. He was a tech executive who needed to conduct sensitive business from home." Tori opened the door to a
small conference room adjacent to the main office. "This room is completely soundproof and has its own climate control system."

Elena stepped into the conference room, and Tori followed, still talking about the room's features. She didn't notice Elena's hand moving to her purse, or the way her client's posture had shifted from casual interest to predatory focus.

"It really is perfect," Elena said softly, and something in her tone made Tori turn around.

That was when she saw the gun.

"I'm sorry, Tori," Elena said, and for a moment, her expression seemed genuinely regretful. "But this isn't about the house."

Chapter 2: Ordinary Moments

Marcus Sterling's office occupied the entire forty-second floor of the Columbia Center, offering a panoramic view of Elliott Bay and the Olympic Mountains beyond. The space reflected his success without ostentation – clean lines, quality materials, and carefully chosen art that spoke of sophistication rather than wealth. He'd learned long ago that the most effective power was the kind that didn't need to announce itself.

The morning conference call with investors had gone well. The downtown sustainable housing project was moving forward on schedule, with groundbreaking planned for the following month. It was the kind of development Marcus took particular pride in – transforming an underutilized urban area into vibrant, environmentally conscious housing that would serve the community for generations.

But as he reviewed construction timelines and permit applications, his mind kept drifting to Tori and her showing at the Whitmore property. The feeling of unease that had nagged at him during breakfast hadn't dissipated. If anything, it had grown stronger as the morning progressed.

"Mr. Sterling?" His assistant, Jennifer, appeared in the doorway with a stack of documents requiring his signature. "The architectural plans for the Belltown project are ready for your review, and the city planning committee wants to schedule another meeting about the environmental impact study."

"Thanks, Jen. Just leave them on my desk. I'll get to them this afternoon." Marcus glanced at his watch. It was nearly eleven-thirty, which meant Tori's showing should be well underway. He considered calling her, then dismissed the idea. She hated being interrupted during client meetings, and he had no rational reason for his concern.

Jennifer hesitated in the doorway. "Is everything alright? You seem a little distracted today."

Marcus had worked with Jennifer for three years, and she'd developed an uncanny ability to read his moods. It was both helpful and occasionally inconvenient, especially when he was trying to maintain the carefully constructed normalcy of his civilian life.

"Just thinking about a project," he said, which was technically true. Tori was the most important project of his life – building a marriage, creating a future, maintaining the illusion that Marcus Sterling was exactly who he appeared to be.

"Well, don't forget you have lunch with the mayor at one o'clock. Something about the waterfront development proposal."

"Right. Thanks for the reminder." Marcus turned back to his computer, but the financial projections on his screen might as well have been written in hieroglyphics. His concentration was shot, and he knew from experience that fighting it would only make things worse.

He pulled out his phone and scrolled to Tori's contact information. Her photo smiled back at him – a candid shot he'd taken during their vacation to Tuscany the previous year. She was laughing at something he'd said, her hair catching the golden light of the Italian sunset, and she looked absolutely radiant. It was his favorite picture of her, capturing not just her beauty but the joy that seemed to radiate from her very being.

Marcus started to dial her number, then stopped. What would he say? That he had a bad feeling? That some instinct he couldn't explain was telling him something was wrong? Tori would listen patiently, reassure him that everything was fine, and then spend the rest of the day worrying that he was becoming overprotective.

Instead, he opened his laptop and pulled up the listing information for the Whitmore property. The photos showed a stunning modern home with all the luxury amenities that attracted Tori's high-end clientele. The location was indeed isolated, situated on a private road with no immediate neighbors. The kind of place where someone could scream and no one would hear.

Marcus shook his head, annoyed with himself for the dark turn his thoughts had taken. This was exactly the kind of paranoid thinking he'd worked so hard to leave behind. Tori was a successful professional showing a house to a legitimate client. The fact that his former life had trained him to see threats everywhere didn't mean those threats actually existed.

He forced himself to focus on the Belltown project plans, losing himself in the technical details of sustainable construction and urban planning. Work had always been his refuge, a way to channel his energy into something constructive and meaningful. The housing crisis in Seattle was real and immediate, and his company was positioned to make a genuine difference in people's lives.

By the time Jennifer knocked on his door to remind him about lunch with the mayor, Marcus had managed to push his concerns about Tori to the back of his mind. The meeting was important – the city was considering several proposals for waterfront development, and Sterling Development Group had submitted what

Marcus believed was the most innovative and environmentally responsible plan.

"I'll be back by three," he told Jennifer as he gathered his materials for the lunch meeting. "If Tori calls, put her through immediately."

"Of course. Should I reschedule your four o'clock if the lunch runs long?"

"No, I'll be back in time." Marcus paused at the door, his hand on the handle. "Actually, if you don't hear from me by two-thirty, call my cell. I don't want to keep the mayor waiting, but I also don't want to cut the conversation short if it's going well."

Jennifer nodded, making a note in her ever-present planner. "Got it. Have a good lunch."

The restaurant Marcus had chosen for the lunch meeting was one of his favorites – a small, intimate place in Pioneer Square that served excellent food without the pretension that often accompanied high-end dining in the city. Mayor Patricia Hendricks was already waiting when he arrived, reviewing what appeared to be policy documents while sipping a glass of sparkling water.

"Marcus, good to see you," she said, rising to shake his hand. Patricia was in her mid fifties, a former city council member who had won the mayor's office on a platform of sustainable development and affordable housing. She and Marcus had worked together on several projects over the years, and he respected both her intelligence and her commitment to the city's long-term welfare.

"Thanks for making time in your schedule, Patricia. I know how busy things get as we head into budget season."

They settled into their seats, and Marcus found himself relaxing for the first time all day. This was his element – discussing projects that mattered, working with people who shared his vision for the city's future, building something lasting and meaningful. It was a far cry from his previous life, where success was measured in missions completed and threats neutralized rather than communities improved and lives enhanced.

"I've been reviewing your waterfront proposal," Patricia said as they ordered their meals. "It's ambitious, but I think it could be exactly what we need to revitalize that area without displacing the existing community."

"That's always been my goal. Development should enhance neighborhoods, not destroy them." Marcus pulled out his tablet to show her the latest renderings. "We've incorporated feedback from the community meetings and adjusted the design to include more affordable housing units and public green space."

As they discussed the technical details of the project, Marcus felt his phone buzz with a text message. He ignored it initially, not wanting to be rude during such an important meeting. But when it buzzed again a few minutes later, he glanced at the screen.

The messages weren't from Tori. They were from Jennifer: "Tori called the office looking for you. Said she tried your cell but it went to voicemail. She sounded a little stressed but said it wasn't urgent."

Marcus frowned. His phone was on silent, but he should have felt it vibrating if Tori had called. He checked his recent calls and saw nothing from her number.

"I'm sorry, Patricia, but could you excuse me for just a moment? I need to check on something."

"Of course."

Marcus stepped outside the restaurant and immediately called Tori's number. It went straight to voicemail, which was unusual. Tori always kept her phone charged and rarely let it die during business hours.

"Hi, you've reached Victoria Sterling with Sterling & Associates. I'm either with a client or away from my phone, but please leave a detailed message and I'll get back to you as soon as possible."

"Tori, it's me. Jennifer said you called the office looking for me. I'm at lunch with the mayor, but call me back as soon as you get this. Love you."

He tried calling again with the same result, then sent a text message: "Got your message. Call me when you can. Everything okay?"

Back inside the restaurant, Marcus attempted to focus on his conversation with Patricia, but his attention kept drifting to his phone. The mayor noticed his distraction and eventually suggested they continue their discussion later in the week.

"I can see you have something on your mind," she said kindly. "Why don't we schedule a follow-up meeting when you can give the project your full attention?"

"I appreciate your understanding. It's probably nothing, but my wife was supposed to call and I haven't heard from her."

"Family comes first," Patricia said firmly. "That's one of the things I've always admired about you, Marcus. You've never let success go to your head or forgotten what really matters."

If only she knew, Marcus thought as they parted ways outside the restaurant. Success in his previous career had required him to forget what mattered, to compartmentalize his emotions and focus solely on the mission. It had taken years of conscious effort to learn how to be a husband, how to let someone else's welfare matter more than his own survival.

The drive back to his office took twenty minutes, during which Marcus tried calling Tori three more times. Each call went straight to voicemail, and his text messages remained unanswered. By the time he reached the Columbia Center, the unease he'd felt that morning had transformed into something approaching panic.

"Any word from Tori?" he asked Jennifer as soon as he walked into the office.

"Nothing since that first call around noon. She said she

was at the property showing and would try to reach you later." Jennifer studied his face with concern. "Marcus, what's wrong? You look like you've seen a ghost."

"I'm sure it's nothing. Her phone probably died, or she's in an area with poor reception." But even as he said the words, Marcus didn't believe them. Tori was meticulous about keeping her phone charged, and the Whitmore property was in an area with excellent cellular coverage.

He tried calling the listing agent for the property, thinking perhaps there had been some change in the showing schedule. The call went to voicemail. He tried the property management company that maintained the house. Same result.

Marcus stood at his office window, looking out at the city spread below him, and felt the familiar sensation of pieces clicking into place. It was a skill he'd developed during his years with the CIA – the ability to recognize patterns, to sense when seemingly unrelated events were actually connected.

Tori's excitement about a new client. Elena Vasquez, with her international business background and interest in privacy features. The isolated location of the Whitmore property. Tori's unusual call to his office, followed by complete radio silence.

He pulled out his phone and scrolled through his contacts until he found a number he hadn't called in over two years. Sarah Chen had been his handler during his final years with the Agency, and she'd helped him establish his new identity when he decided to leave that life behind. She now ran a private security firm in D.C., and she was one of only three people in the world who knew that Marcus Sterling had once been someone else entirely.

The phone rang twice before Sarah's familiar voice answered. "Well, well. Phoenix calling after all this time. This can't be good news."

"Sarah, I need a favor. A big one."

"I figured as much. You wouldn't be calling otherwise. What's the situation?"

Marcus took a deep breath, knowing that making this call would change everything. Once he involved Sarah, there would be no going back to the comfortable fiction that he was just a successful real estate developer with a normal life and a normal marriage.

"I think someone from the old days has found me.

And I think they have my wife."

Chapter 3: The Trap Springs

The gun in Elena's hand was small but unmistakably lethal – a compact pistol that spoke of professional training and serious intent. Tori's mind struggled to process what she was seeing, her brain refusing to accept that her routine property showing had transformed into something from a nightmare.

"I don't understand," Tori said, her voice barely above a whisper. The professional confidence that had carried her through hundreds of client meetings evaporated, replaced by a primal fear that made her hands shake. "What do you want? If this is about money, I can—"

"This isn't about money," Elena interrupted, her accent more pronounced now that she'd dropped the pretense of being a potential buyer. "And I'm truly sorry it has to be this way. You seem like a genuinely nice person, and under different circumstances, I think we might have been friends."

"Then why?" Tori's eyes darted around the conference room, looking for an escape route or something she could use as a weapon. But Elena had chosen her location well – they were in the most isolated part of an already isolated house, with no neighbors close enough to hear a scream and no easy way out.

"Because your husband isn't who you think he is," Elena said, her dark eyes never leaving Tori's face. "And the only way to draw him out is to take something he values more than his own life."

The words hit Tori like a physical blow. "Marcus? What does Marcus have to do with this? He's a real estate developer. He builds affordable housing and sustainable communities. He's never hurt anyone in his life."

Elena's laugh was bitter, tinged with pain that seemed to come from somewhere deep inside her. "Marcus Sterling might never have hurt anyone. But the man you married used to go by a different name, and he's responsible for destroying my family."

"You're insane." Tori took a step backward, her mind racing. The conference room had only one door, and Elena was blocking it. The windows were floor-to-ceiling but didn't open – a security feature that now trapped her as effectively as prison bars.

"Am I? Tell me, Tori, what do you really know about your husband's past? What did he do before he started Sterling Development Group? Where did he get the capital to launch such an ambitious company? What happened to his family, his childhood friends, his college roommates?"

Each question was like a small knife, cutting into Tori's certainty about the man she'd married. She realized with growing horror that she couldn't answer any of them. Marcus had always been vague about his past, claiming it was too painful to discuss. She'd assumed he was an orphan or had come from a troubled family, and she'd never pushed for details out of respect for his privacy.

"He told me his parents died when he was young," Tori said, but even as she spoke, she could hear the uncertainty in her own voice.

"Maybe they did. Or maybe that's just another lie in a life built on deception." Elena's gun never wavered, but her expression softened slightly. "I know this is hard to hear. I know you love him. But the man you married is a killer, Tori. A professional killer who worked for the

CIA for over a decade."

"No." The word came out as a sob. "No, that's not possible. Marcus is gentle. He's kind. He rescues spiders from the bathtub instead of killing them. He cries during sad movies. He's not a killer."

"People can be many things," Elena said quietly. "The capacity for violence doesn't negate the capacity for love. I'm sure he does love you, in his way. But that doesn't change what he's done."

Tori's legs felt weak, and she sank into one of the conference room chairs. The elegant furniture that had seemed so impressive an hour ago now felt like props in a surreal play where she'd been cast in a role she didn't understand.

"What do you want from him?" she asked, her voice hollow.

"Justice. Closure. An end to the nightmares that have haunted me for eight years." Elena moved closer, but kept the gun trained on Tori. "Your husband led a mission that destroyed an arms dealing operation in Eastern Europe. In the process, he killed my brother."

"If your brother was an arms dealer—"

"My brother was nineteen years old and had never held a gun in his life," Elena snapped, her composure cracking for the first time. "He was a college student who happened to be in the wrong place at the wrong time. Your husband put two bullets in his chest and left him to die in a warehouse in Prague."

Tori stared at Elena, seeing the pain that radiated from her like heat from a fire. Whether or not her story was true, Elena believed it completely. The grief and rage that drove her were real, even if her facts might be distorted by trauma and time.

"Even if that's true," Tori said carefully, "it doesn't justify this. Kidnapping me won't bring your brother back."

"No, but it will bring your husband to me. And when he comes – and he will come, because despite everything else, I believe he really does love you – we'll finally have our reckoning."

Elena reached into her purse with her free hand and pulled out a small device that looked like a modified cell phone. "This is going to send a very specific message to your husband. It will tell him that his past has caught up with him and that he has twenty-four hours to come alone to a location I'll specify later."

"And if he doesn't come?"

Elena's expression hardened. "Then you'll pay the price for his sins. But he'll come, Tori. Men like your husband – men who've spent their lives in the shadows – they understand the rules of this game better than anyone."

"What rules?" Tori asked, though she wasn't sure she wanted to know the answer.

"The rule that says the innocent suffer for the crimes of the guilty. The rule that says the past never stays buried. The rule that says everyone eventually pays for what they've done." Elena pressed a button on the device, and Tori heard a faint electronic beep. "There. The message is sent. Now we wait."

"Wait for what?"

"For your husband to remember who he really is. For Phoenix to rise from the ashes of Marcus Sterling's carefully constructed life." Elena gestured toward the door with her gun. "We're going to take a little trip now. Somewhere more secure, where your husband and I can have our conversation without interruption."

Tori stood on unsteady legs, her mind still reeling from Elena's revelations. "Where are you taking me?"

"Somewhere your husband will find us when he's ready. Somewhere with enough privacy for what needs to happen." Elena opened the conference room door and motioned for Tori to walk ahead of her. "Don't try anything heroic. I don't want to hurt you, but I will if you force me to."

As they walked through the Whitmore house, Tori found herself seeing the property with new eyes. The isolation that had been a selling point now felt ominous. The security features that were meant to protect the owners now served to conceal a crime. The beautiful architecture that had impressed so many clients now seemed like an elaborate stage set for a tragedy.

"My car or yours?" Elena asked as they reached the front door.

"What?"

"We need to leave your car here so your husband will know you were taken from this location. We'll take mine." Elena opened the front door and gestured for Tori to step outside. "The black sedan. Move slowly and keep your hands where I can see them."

The afternoon sun felt surreal on Tori's face, as if she were experiencing it through a thick pane of glass. Everything looked normal – the manicured landscaping, the circular driveway, the view of Lake Washington through the trees. But nothing would ever be normal again.

Elena's car was expensive and nondescript, the kind of vehicle that wouldn't attract attention in any neighborhood. The interior was immaculate, with no personal items visible. It was the car of someone who lived carefully, someone who planned for contingencies.

"Seatbelt," Elena said as she started the engine. "I don't want you getting hurt in an accident. That would complicate things unnecessarily."

As they drove away from the Whitmore property, Tori watched the familiar landscape of Mercer Island pass by the window. She thought about Marcus, probably sitting in his office reviewing construction plans or meeting with investors. Did he know yet that something was wrong? Had he received Elena's message?

"How long have you been planning this?" Tori asked.

"Two years of active preparation. Eight years of

waiting for the right opportunity." Elena navigated through traffic with the same calm efficiency she'd shown during their

house tour. "Your husband is very good at hiding, but everyone makes mistakes eventually. He made his when he fell in love with you."

"Love isn't a mistake."

"It is when you're trying to disappear from people who want you dead." Elena glanced at Tori in the rearview mirror. "He should have stayed alone. Should have kept moving, kept changing identities. Instead, he got comfortable. He built a life, established routines, created vulnerabilities."

"You mean me."

"You're his greatest vulnerability and his greatest strength. The thing that makes him most human and most dangerous." Elena turned onto the interstate, heading north toward the mountains. "That's why this will work. He'll come for you, and when he does, he'll be thinking with his heart instead of his head."

Tori closed her eyes, trying to process everything that had happened in the past hour. This morning, she'd been a successful real estate agent married to a loving husband, looking forward to a routine day of showings and paperwork. Now she was a kidnapping victim, learning that her entire marriage might be built on lies.

But even as doubt crept into her mind, Tori found herself clinging to what she knew about Marcus. The way he held her when she had nightmares. The patience he showed when she was stressed about work. The gentle way he touched her face when he thought she was sleeping. Those moments couldn't be fabricated. Whatever he might have done in his past, the man she'd married was real.

"He'll come for me," she said quietly.

"I'm counting on it," Elena replied. "And when he does, we'll finally learn whether Marcus Sterling is strong enough to survive the return of Phoenix."

As the car climbed into the Cascade Mountains, Tori watched Seattle disappear in the distance and wondered if she would ever see her home again. Somewhere behind them, Marcus was about to discover that his carefully constructed new life was about to collide with the ghosts of his past.

The game, as Elena had called it, was about to begin.

Chapter 4: Missing

The silence on the other end of the phone was more terrifying than any scream could have been. Sarah Chen had been Marcus's handler for three years during his time with the Agency, and she'd never been at a loss for words. The fact that she was quiet now meant she was processing the implications of what he'd just told her, running through scenarios and calculating risks with the same methodical precision that had made her one of the CIA's most effective operations managers.

"How long has she been missing?" Sarah finally asked, her voice taking on the crisp, professional tone Marcus remembered from their operational briefings.

"Four hours since her last known contact. Maybe five." Marcus paced behind his desk, every instinct screaming at him to take action while his rational mind insisted on gathering more information first. "She called the office looking for me around noon, but I was in a meeting. Since then, nothing. Phone goes straight to voicemail, text messages unanswered."

"Could be innocent. Dead battery, car trouble, extended client meeting."

"Not Tori. She's obsessive about staying in touch, especially when she's showing properties in isolated areas." Marcus stopped pacing and stared out at the Seattle skyline, seeing nothing but the reflection of his own fears in the glass. "And there's something else. The client she was meeting – Elena Vasquez. International business, import-export, new to the area. It fits the profile."

"Profile for what?"

"Someone with the resources and motivation to track down a former CIA operative who's been off the grid for seven years." Marcus pulled up the property listing on his computer, studying the photos of the Whitmore house with new eyes. "The location is perfect for an ambush. Isolated, private road, no neighbors within screaming distance."

Sarah was quiet for another long moment, and Marcus could almost hear her mental gears turning. She'd always been three steps ahead of everyone else in the room, anticipating problems before they materialized and developing contingency plans for situations that might never arise.

"Assuming you're right," she said carefully, "assuming someone from the old days has found you, what's their endgame? Revenge? Information? Leverage for something bigger?"

"I don't know. That's what scares me." Marcus sat down heavily in his chair, feeling the weight of seven years of carefully constructed normalcy crashing down around him. "I've been out of the game for so long, Sarah. I don't know who might still be carrying grudges or what operations might have had delayed consequences."

"The Prague job."

The words hit Marcus like a physical blow. Prague had been his last mission, the one that had finally convinced him to leave the Agency and disappear into civilian life. It had been a textbook operation on paper – infiltrate an arms dealing network, gather intelligence, neutralize the threat. But textbook operations had a way of becoming complicated when real people with real lives got caught in the crossfire.

"Viktor Kozlov's operation," Marcus said, the name tasting bitter in his mouth. "We took down his entire network, seized millions in weapons, cash, and arrested half his organization."

"And killed his son in the process."

"Alexei Kozlov was armed and shooting at federal agents. It was a clean kill, Sarah. Justified and necessary."

"I know that. You know that. But Viktor Kozlov is a father who lost his child, and fathers don't always care about the legal niceties of justified force." Sarah's voice softened slightly. "How much does Tori know about your past?"

"Nothing. She thinks I'm exactly who I appear to be – a real estate developer who grew up in foster care and built his business from nothing." Marcus felt a familiar stab of guilt at the deception, even though he'd told himself a thousand times that it was necessary to protect both of them. "She's never asked too many questions, and I've never volunteered information."

"That might actually work in our favor. If whoever has her thinks she knows about your CIA background, they might keep her alive longer to use as leverage. If they realize she's genuinely innocent, they might..." Sarah didn't finish the sentence, but Marcus understood the implication.

"I need to find her, Sarah. Whatever it takes."

"I know you do. And I'm going to help you. But we need to be smart about this. If you go charging in like some kind of action hero, you'll get both of you killed." The sound of typing came through the phone as Sarah accessed databases that officially didn't exist. "Give me everything you know about this Elena Vasquez. Physical description, accent, any details about her supposed business."

Marcus closed his eyes and tried to remember everything Tori had told him about her new client. "Late twenties, dark hair, well-dressed, professional demeanor. Slight accent that Tori couldn't place. Said she was in import-export, relocating from New York, had the financial backing for a twelve-million-dollar purchase."

"Import-export is a classic cover for intelligence operatives. Gives them a reason to travel internationally and maintain contacts in multiple countries." More typing. "I'm running facial recognition on the security cameras at the Whitmore property. If this Elena is who we think she is, she'll be in the system somewhere."

"How long will that take?"

"Give me an hour. Maybe two if the cameras are on a

closed system." Sarah paused. "Marcus, I need you to listen to me very carefully. Do not contact the police. Do not involve local law enforcement. If this is connected to your past, bringing in civilians will only get more people killed."

"There's already a detective involved. Ray Morrison, Seattle PD. He's the one who would catch the case when Tori is officially reported missing."

"How well do you know him?"

"Well enough. We've worked together on some community development projects. He's a good cop, former military, understands the importance of operational security." Marcus considered his options. "I think I can trust him with part of the truth. Not everything, but enough to get his cooperation."

"Be very careful what you tell him. The fewer people who know about your background, the better." Sarah's tone became more urgent. "I'm going to make some calls, reach out to some contacts who might have heard chatter about operations targeting former Agency personnel. In the meantime, you need to start thinking like Phoenix again."

The name hit Marcus like a cold wind, bringing back memories he'd worked hard to suppress. Phoenix had been his operational codename, chosen because of his ability to rise from the ashes of blown covers and failed missions. He'd been good at his job – maybe too good – and that skill had come at a cost he was still paying.

"I'm not sure I remember how," he admitted.

"It's like riding a bicycle. The training never really leaves you, it just gets buried under layers of civilian life." Sarah's voice took on the commanding tone he remembered from their operational briefings. "Start with the basics. Assume your home is compromised, your communications are monitored, your normal routines are being watched. Think like a target, because that's what you are now."

Marcus looked around his office with new eyes, seeing potential surveillance points and escape routes instead of the comfortable workspace he'd created. The transformation was unsettling, like watching his carefully constructed life dissolve before his eyes.

"What about Tori? How do I find her?"

"We start with the assumption that whoever has her wants you to find them. This isn't a random kidnapping for ransom – it's a trap designed to draw you out.

They'll make contact soon, probably with demands or conditions for her release."

"And when they do?"

"We'll be ready. But Marcus, you need to understand something. The man who can save Tori isn't Marcus Sterling, successful businessman and loving husband. It's Phoenix, and Phoenix was a killer. Are you prepared to become that person again?"

Marcus stared at his reflection in the office window, seeing a stranger looking back at him. The face was the same, but something had changed in his eyes. The careful control he'd maintained for seven years was cracking, revealing glimpses of the man he used to be.

"For Tori? I'll become whoever I need to be."

"Good. Because Phoenix is going to need every skill he ever learned to bring her home alive." Sarah's voice softened again. "I'll call you as soon as I have something. And Marcus? We're going to get her back. I promise."

The line went dead, leaving Marcus alone with his thoughts and the growing certainty that his old life was about to collide with his new one in the most violent way possible. He pulled out his phone and scrolled to

Detective Morrison's number, knowing that the next call he made would set events in motion that couldn't be undone.

But first, he needed to go home and prepare for war.

The drive from downtown Seattle to his house in Bellevue normally took Marcus forty five minutes in evening traffic. Today, he made it in twenty-five, his mind focused on the tactical considerations of what lay ahead. If Sarah was right, if this was connected to his CIA past, then his home was no longer a sanctuary. It was a potential battlefield.

He parked in the garage and entered through the kitchen, moving with the careful awareness that had once been second nature. Every shadow could conceal a threat, every sound could signal danger. The comfortable familiarity of his home felt alien now, as if he were seeing it through the eyes of a stranger.

The first thing he noticed was that nothing had been disturbed. If Elena or her associates had been here, they'd been careful to leave no trace. But Marcus hadn't survived ten years in the intelligence community by taking things at face value. He moved through the house systematically, checking for signs of surveillance or intrusion that a civilian would never notice.

In his study, he found what he was looking for. The books on his shelf had been moved – not obviously, but enough that someone with his training would notice. Someone had been here, searching for information about his past or clues to his current activities. They'd been professional about it, but not quite professional enough.

Marcus went to his desk and opened the bottom drawer, reaching behind the hanging files to find the small metal box he'd hoped never to touch again. Inside were items from his previous life: a passport in a name that wasn't Marcus Sterling, a credit card linked to an account in the Cayman Islands, and a Glock 19 that had saved his life more times than he cared to remember.

The gun felt strange in his hands after seven years of civilian life, but the muscle memory was still there. He checked the magazine, chambered a round, and tucked the weapon into the waistband of his pants. Phoenix was beginning to emerge from the ashes of Marcus Sterling's carefully constructed identity.

His phone rang, startling him from his preparations.

The caller ID showed Detective Morrison's number.

"Morrison."

"Detective, it's Marcus Sterling. I need to report my wife missing."

"Marcus? What's going on? When did you last see her?"

"This morning. She had a property showing on Mercer Island, and she hasn't been in contact since noon. Her phone goes straight to voicemail, and she's missed several appointments." Marcus forced himself to sound like a concerned husband rather than a former intelligence operative. "This isn't like her, Ray. Something's wrong."

"Okay, slow down. Give me the details. Where was the showing, who was the client, what time was she supposed to be back?"

Marcus provided the information, carefully editing out his suspicions about Elena's true identity. Morrison was a good detective, but he wasn't equipped to handle the kind of threat that Marcus suspected they were facing.

"I'll head over to the property now and take a look around," Morrison said. "Can you meet me there?"

"I'm on my way."

As Marcus prepared to leave, his phone buzzed with a text message from an unknown number: "Your wife is safe for now. Come alone to the coordinates I'm sending, and she stays that way. Bring backup, and she dies. You have 24 hours to decide if you're still the man you used to be. - A friend from Prague"

The message was followed by GPS coordinates that Marcus recognized as a location in the Cascade Mountains, about two hours northeast of Seattle. Remote, isolated, perfect for the kind of confrontation that someone from his past might want to arrange.

Marcus stared at the message, feeling the last vestiges of his civilian life slip away. Marcus Sterling would have called the police, would have followed proper procedures and trusted in the system to protect his wife. But Phoenix knew better. Phoenix understood that some battles could only be fought in the shadows, and some enemies could only be defeated by becoming more ruthless than they were.

He deleted the message and headed for his car, knowing that when he returned, either both he and Tori would be alive, or neither of them would be. There was no middle ground in the world he was about to re-enter.

The game, as Elena had called it, was about to begin in earnest.

Chapter 5: Ghosts of the Past

The Whitmore property looked different in the fading light of evening, its modern architecture casting sharp shadows across the manicured landscape. Detective Ray Morrison's unmarked sedan was already parked in the circular driveway when Marcus arrived, and he could see the detective's flashlight beam moving through the interior of the house.

Marcus sat in his car for a moment, steeling himself for what he was about to do. Involving Morrison was a risk, but it was also necessary. He needed someone with official authority to document Tori's disappearance and provide cover for his own actions. The trick would be giving the detective enough information to be useful without revealing the full scope of what they were dealing with.

"Marcus!" Morrison called out as he emerged from the house. "I've been through the whole place. No signs of struggle, no obvious evidence of foul play. Her car's here, keys still in the ignition, purse on the front seat."

"What about security cameras?"

"That's the interesting part. The system was disabled around two o'clock this afternoon. Someone who knew what they were doing accessed the control panel and shut it down." Morrison studied Marcus's face in the dim light. "You said your wife was meeting a client named Elena Vasquez?"

"That's right. Import-export business, relocating from New York." Marcus followed Morrison toward the house, his trained eyes automatically cataloging potential surveillance points and escape routes. "She seemed legitimate when Tori described her. Asked all the right questions, had the financial backing for this kind of purchase."

"I ran the name through our databases. No hits, which could mean she's clean or it could mean she's using an alias." Morrison led Marcus into the conference room where Tori had been taken. "This is where I think it happened. The chairs are positioned like two people were having a conversation, and there are some scuff marks on the floor that suggest movement."

Marcus knelt down and examined the marks, his mind automatically reconstructing the scene. Tori had been sitting in the chair facing the door, probably relaxed and professional. Elena had been in the chair with her back to the window, controlling the exit and maintaining tactical advantage. The scuff marks suggested Tori had stood up quickly, possibly in response to a threat.

"Any witnesses? Other agents showing properties in the area?"

"I'm checking with the other real estate offices, but this road is pretty isolated. The nearest neighbor is half a mile away and was at work all day." Morrison watched Marcus examine the scene with growing curiosity. "You seem to know what you're looking for."

"I watch a lot of crime shows," Marcus said, which was technically true even if it wasn't the whole truth. "What's the next step?"

"Officially? We wait twenty-four hours before filing a missing person report. Unofficially? I'm treating this as a potential kidnapping from the moment we walk out of here." Morrison's expression was grim. "The disabled security system changes everything. This wasn't random."

Marcus's phone buzzed with a text message, and his blood ran cold when he saw it was from the same unknown number that had contacted him earlier: "Enjoying your visit to the crime scene? Your detective friend seems competent, but he's out of his league. This is between you and me, Phoenix. Don't make me prove how serious I am."

"Everything okay?" Morrison asked, noticing Marcus's expression.

"Just work stuff. Crisis at one of my construction sites." Marcus forced himself to look calm while his mind raced. Whoever had Tori was watching them right now, which meant they had surveillance on the property. Professional surveillance that Morrison wouldn't detect without specialized equipment.

"We should go," Marcus said. "There's nothing more to learn here, and I want to get home in case Tori tries to call."

Morrison nodded, but Marcus could see the detective's instincts were telling him something was wrong. Ray Morrison hadn't survived twenty years in law enforcement
by ignoring his gut feelings, and right now his gut was probably screaming that Marcus Sterling wasn't telling him everything.

As they walked back to their cars, Morrison stopped and turned to face Marcus directly. "I need to ask you something, and I want a straight answer. Is there anything in your past or Tori's past that might explain this? Any enemies, any business deals gone wrong, any reason someone might target your family?"

The question hung in the air between them, and Marcus felt the weight of seven years of carefully constructed lies pressing down on him. Morrison deserved the truth, or at least part of it. But the truth would put the detective in danger and potentially compromise any chance of getting Tori back alive.

"Nothing I can think of," Marcus said finally. "We live quiet lives, Ray. Tori sells houses, I build them. We don't have enemies."

Morrison studied his face for a long moment, and Marcus could see the detective filing away his suspicions for later investigation. "Alright. But if you think of anything – anything at all – you call me immediately. And Marcus? Don't try to handle this yourself. Whatever's going on here, it's bigger than a missing person case."

"I understand."

But as Marcus drove away from the Whitmore property, he knew that understanding and compliance were two very different things. Morrison was a good cop and a decent man, but he lived in a world where problems were solved through proper procedures and legal channels. The world Marcus was about to re-enter operated by different rules entirely.

His phone rang as he merged onto the interstate, and Sarah Chen's number appeared on the display.

"I've got something," she said without preamble. "Elena Vasquez is an alias, but a good one. Took me three hours and some favors I'd rather not have called in to crack it."

"Who is she really?"

"Elena Kozlov. Viktor's daughter, though she's been using her mother's maiden name since she was eighteen. Graduated from Columbia with a degree in international relations, speaks four languages fluently, and has been off the grid for the past two years."

The name hit Marcus like a physical blow. Viktor Kozlov's daughter. The arms dealer whose son he'd killed in Prague had a daughter, and she'd spent years preparing for this moment.

"What else do you know about her?"

"She's smart, well-trained, and has access to resources that most people can only dream of. Her father may be a criminal, but he's a wealthy criminal with connections throughout Eastern Europe and beyond." Sarah's voice was tense. "Marcus, this isn't just about revenge. This is about family honor, about a daughter avenging her brother's death. She won't stop until one of you is dead."

"Then I'll make sure it's her."

"It's not that simple. Elena isn't some street thug with a grudge. She's been planning this for years, and she's had professional training. The kind of training that makes her almost as dangerous as you used to be."

Marcus thought about the text message, about the surveillance that had tracked his movements to the crime scene. Elena was indeed professional, but she'd also made a mistake. She'd revealed her emotional investment in the outcome, and emotion was a weakness that could be exploited.

"What about Viktor? Is he involved in this directly?"

"Unknown. My sources suggest he's been keeping a

low profile since Prague, rebuilding his organization and staying out of international law enforcement's crosshairs. But funding his daughter's revenge operation? That would be exactly his style."

Marcus pulled into his driveway and sat in the darkness of his garage, processing the information. Elena Kozlov had his wife, and she wanted him to come to her on her terms. It was a trap, obviously, but it was also his only chance to get Tori back alive.

"I need equipment," he said. "Weapons, surveillance gear, communications equipment. The kind of stuff that isn't available at your local sporting goods store."

"I figured you might. There's a storage unit in Tacoma, about thirty minutes south of your location. Unit 247 at SecureSpace Storage on Pacific Avenue. The access code is your old badge number." Sarah paused. "Everything you need should be there, plus some things you probably don't remember stashing away."
"You've been planning for this."

"I've been planning for the possibility that your past might catch up with you. It's what good handlers do – we prepare for contingencies that we hope never happen." Sarah's voice softened slightly. "Marcus, I need you to understand something. The equipment in that storage unit will turn you back into Phoenix, but Phoenix was a killer. Once you cross that line, there's no going back to being just Marcus Sterling."

"Tori is worth crossing any line."

"I know she is. That's what makes you dangerous and what makes you vulnerable. Elena is counting on your love for your wife to make you reckless. Don't give her that advantage."

"What do you suggest?"

"Be smart. Be patient. Be the professional you used to be, not the desperate husband you are now." Sarah's tone became businesslike again. "I'm flying out to Seattle tonight. I should be there by morning, and I'll bring some additional resources that might be useful."

"Sarah, you don't have to—"

"Yes, I do. You were my best operative, and Tori is an innocent civilian caught up in something that started long before she met you. We're going to get her back, and we're going to make sure Elena Kozlov never threatens anyone again."

After Sarah hung up, Marcus sat in his car and tried to prepare himself mentally for what lay ahead. In a few hours, he would drive to Tacoma and reclaim the tools of his former trade. He would transform himself from Marcus Sterling, loving husband and successful businessman, into Phoenix, the CIA operative who had once been feared throughout the international intelligence community.

But first, he needed to say goodbye to the life he was about to leave behind.

Inside the house, Marcus moved through the rooms he and Tori had made into a home, touching objects that held memories of their five years together. The coffee mug she'd used that morning, still sitting in the sink. The book she'd been reading, left open on her nightstand with a bookmark marking her place. The framed photo of their wedding day, both of them laughing at something the photographer had said.

In their bedroom, Marcus opened the closet and pulled out a small velvet box from behind Tori's shoe collection. Inside was the necklace he'd planned to give her for their upcoming anniversary – a delicate chain with a pendant shaped like a phoenix rising from flames. He'd chosen it because it represented rebirth and new beginnings, the chance to build something beautiful from the ashes of a difficult past.

Now the symbolism felt ominous, as if he'd somehow

predicted this moment when his old life would consume his new one.

Marcus put the necklace in his pocket and walked to his study, where he sat down to write a letter he hoped Tori would never have to read. If something went wrong, if he didn't survive the confrontation with Elena, he wanted his wife to know the truth about who he'd been and why he'd kept it from her.

"My dearest Tori," he began, and then stopped, unsure how to explain a lifetime of deception in a few paragraphs. How could he make her understand that every lie had been told out of love, every secret kept to protect her from a world she should never have to know existed?

In the end, he wrote simply and honestly, telling her about Phoenix and the CIA, about Prague and Viktor Kozlov, about the choices he'd made and the prices he'd paid. He told her that loving her had been the best decision of his life, and that becoming Marcus Sterling had been worth every sacrifice.

He sealed the letter in an envelope and left it on his desk, hoping she would find it someday and understand. Then he gathered his courage and prepared to become Phoenix one last time.

The storage unit in Tacoma was exactly where Sarah had said it would be, tucked away in an industrial complex that most people drove past without noticing. Marcus used his old badge number to access the facility and found unit 247 in the back corner, away from the main traffic patterns.

Inside, he found a carefully organized arsenal that represented the tools of his former trade. Weapons, ammunition, surveillance equipment, communications gear, and tactical clothing – everything a professional intelligence operative might need for extended field operations. Sarah had been thorough in her preparations, anticipating needs he might not have considered.

Marcus selected what he would need for the confrontation ahead: a tactical vest, night vision goggles, a sniper rifle with a high-powered scope, and enough ammunition to fight a small war. He also took a secure satellite phone that would allow him to communicate with Sarah without risk of interception.

As he loaded the equipment into his car, Marcus felt the familiar weight of responsibility settling on his shoulders. Phoenix had always worked alone, had always been willing to do whatever was necessary to complete the mission. But this mission was different.

This time, the stakes weren't geopolitical or strategic – they were personal.

Elena Kozlov had his wife, and she wanted him to come to her. He would go, but not as the desperate husband she expected. He would go as Phoenix, and he would remind her why that name had once struck fear into the hearts of his enemies.

The game was about to begin, and Marcus intended to win.

Chapter 6: Old Allies

Sarah Chen stepped off the red-eye flight from Washington D.C. looking exactly as Marcus remembered her – impeccably dressed despite the early hour, alert eyes that missed nothing, and the kind of controlled energy that came from years of managing high-stakes operations. At forty-eight, she moved with the confidence of someone who had earned her position through competence rather than politics, and her presence at Sea-Tac Airport felt like a lifeline to Marcus.

"You look like hell," she said by way of greeting, falling into step beside him as they walked toward the parking garage.

"I feel worse than I look." Marcus had managed perhaps two hours of sleep, his mind too active to allow for rest. Every time he closed his eyes, he saw Tori's face and imagined what Elena might be doing to her. "Any new intelligence?"

"Some. Viktor Kozlov has been more active in the past six months than he's been since Prague. Moving money, making contacts, rebuilding his network." Sarah adjusted her carry-on bag, and Marcus noticed the subtle bulge that suggested she was armed. "My sources think he's been planning something big, but nobody knew what until now."

They reached Marcus's Range Rover, and he noticed Sarah automatically checking the vehicle for signs of tampering before getting in. Old habits died hard in their line of work, and paranoia was often the difference between coming home and disappearing forever.

"What's our tactical situation?" Marcus asked as they drove toward the city.

"Complicated. Elena has chosen her ground well – the coordinates she sent you are for a cabin in the North Cascades, about twenty miles from the nearest town.

Remote, defensible, with multiple escape routes through the mountains." Sarah pulled out a tablet and showed him satellite imagery of the area. "It's also a place where gunfire won't attract attention, and bodies can disappear for years."

Marcus studied the terrain, his mind automatically calculating approach routes and potential ambush points. The cabin sat in a small valley surrounded by dense forest, with a single access road that could easily be monitored or blocked. It was exactly the kind of location he would have chosen for a similar operation.

"She's not planning to let either of us leave alive," he said.

"Probably not. But she's also emotionally invested in this confrontation, which gives us an advantage. Revenge operations are personal, and personal means predictable." Sarah zoomed in on the satellite image. "The question is whether she's working alone or if Viktor sent backup."

"What's your assessment?"

"Elena is smart enough to know she can't take you in a straight fight, even with the element of surprise. She'll have contingencies, probably including remote surveillance and automated defenses." Sarah switched to a different view that showed the surrounding area. "But she's also young and angry, and that combination leads to mistakes."

They drove in silence for a few minutes, both lost in their own thoughts. Marcus found himself remembering the last time he and Sarah had worked together, a counter terrorism operation in Berlin that had required them to trust each other completely. She'd saved his life twice during that mission, and he'd returned the favor once. It was the kind of partnership that only developed between people who had faced death together and survived.

"There's something else," Sarah said as they entered downtown Seattle. "I've been monitoring communications traffic in the area, and there's been an unusual amount of encrypted chatter on frequencies typically used by Eastern European criminal organizations."

"Viktor's people?"

"Possibly. Or it could be unrelated. But the timing is suspicious, and I don't believe in coincidences." Sarah closed her tablet and looked at Marcus directly. "I think

Elena has more support than she's letting on. This might not be just a daughter seeking revenge – it could be the opening move in a larger operation against former CIA personnel."

The possibility sent a chill down Marcus's spine. If Viktor was targeting other former operatives, then Tori's kidnapping was just the beginning. Other families, other innocent people, could be drawn into a war they didn't understand and couldn't fight.

"We need to end this quickly," Marcus said.

"Agreed. But we also need to be smart about it. Elena is expecting you to come charging in like an avenging husband. We need to give her something she's not expecting."

They pulled into the parking garage of Marcus's office building, and Sarah immediately began scanning for potential surveillance. Her training was showing the careful awareness that had kept her alive through fifteen years of intelligence work.

"What did you have in mind?" Marcus asked.

"We make her think she's winning. You go to the meeting as planned, but you don't go alone. I'll be in position to provide overwatch and support." Sarah's smile was predatory. "Elena wants to face Phoenix? Let's give her the full experience."

Marcus's office felt strange with Sarah in it, as if two incompatible worlds were colliding. She moved through the space like a professional, noting sight lines and potential vulnerabilities while maintaining the appearance of a casual business meeting. To anyone watching, she would look like a consultant or potential investor, not a former CIA operations manager planning a rescue mission.

"Nice setup," she said, examining the view from his windows. "Good fields of fire, multiple exit routes, secure communications. You've maintained better operational security than most retirees."
"Old habits."

"Good habits. They might be what keeps you alive." Sarah turned from the window and became all business. "Let's talk equipment. What did you take from the storage unit?"

Marcus showed her the gear he'd selected, and she nodded approvingly at most of his choices. She made a few suggestions for additions – a portable signal jammer, thermal imaging equipment, and a medical kit designed for battlefield trauma.

"You're expecting this to get messy," Marcus observed.

"I'm expecting Elena to be better prepared than she appears. Young doesn't mean inexperienced, and angry doesn't mean stupid." Sarah checked her watch. "We have about eighteen hours before your deadline. That gives us time to scout the location and set up properly."

"What about Tori? Every hour we delay is another hour she's in danger."

"And every minute we rush is another chance for both of you to end up dead. Elena has kept her alive this long because she needs her as bait. She won't kill her before you arrive – it would defeat the purpose of the entire operation."

Marcus knew Sarah was right, but the logical part of his mind was at war with the emotional part that wanted to drive straight to the mountains and tear Elena apart with his bare hands. It was exactly the kind of thinking that got operatives killed, and he forced himself to focus on the tactical requirements of the mission.

"There's something else we need to discuss," Sarah

said, her tone becoming more serious. "What happens after we get Tori back? Elena and Viktor won't just disappear if this operation fails. They'll regroup and try again, and next time they might target other people you care about."

"Then we make sure there isn't a next time."

"That's what I was hoping you'd say." Sarah pulled a file from her bag and set it on Marcus's desk. "I've been putting together intelligence on Viktor's current operation. Financial records, communication intercepts, known associates. Everything we'd need to take down his entire network."

Marcus opened the file and saw the familiar format of an operational briefing – target profiles, asset locations, tactical assessments. It was the kind of comprehensive intelligence package that took months to develop, which meant Sarah had been planning this for longer than she'd admitted.

"How long have you been working on this?"

"Since Prague. I knew Viktor would eventually come for revenge, and I wanted to be ready when he did." Sarah's expression was grim. "He's not just a criminal anymore, Marcus. He's become something worse – a man with nothing left to lose and the resources to act on his hatred."

"So we take him down permanently."

"We take down his entire organization. His financial network, his weapons suppliers, his operational infrastructure. We make sure that when this is over, Viktor Kozlov is just another old man with no power and no way to threaten anyone ever again."

Marcus studied the intelligence files, seeing the scope of what Sarah was proposing. It wasn't just a rescue mission – it was a full-scale covert operation designed to dismantle a criminal empire. The kind of mission that Phoenix had specialized in during his years with the Agency.

"This is bigger than just getting Tori back," he said.

"Yes, it is. But it's also the only way to make sure she stays safe. As long as Viktor has power and resources, he'll keep coming. The only way to protect your family is to eliminate the threat permanently."

Marcus closed the file and looked at Sarah, seeing the determination in her eyes. She'd been his handler, his mentor, and sometimes his conscience during his years as Phoenix. If she thought this was necessary, then it probably was.

"What do you need from me?"

"I need you to be Phoenix one more time. Not just for a few hours, but for as long as it takes to finish this properly." Sarah's voice was steady, but Marcus could hear the weight of what she was asking. "I need you to be the man who could walk into a room full of enemies and walk out alone."

"And after it's over?"

"After it's over, you go back to being Marcus Sterling. You rebuild your life with Tori, and you never have to worry about the past catching up with you again." Sarah stood up and moved to the window, looking out at the city below. "But first, we have to make sure there's an 'after' to go back to."

Marcus's phone buzzed with another message from Elena: "I hope you're not planning anything foolish. Your wife is counting on you to be smart about this. Come alone, as instructed, and she lives. Bring friends, and she dies slowly."

He showed the message to Sarah, who read it with professional detachment.

"She's monitoring your communications," Sarah said. "Which means she probably knows I'm here."

"Is that a problem?"

"It's an opportunity. She thinks she knows what we're planning, but she's only seeing part of the picture." Sarah smiled, and Marcus was reminded of why she'd been so effective as an operations manager. "Let her think she's in control. It will make her overconfident, and overconfidence is a weakness we can exploit."

As they prepared to leave the office, Marcus felt the familiar sensation of pieces falling into place. The mission parameters were clear, the intelligence was solid, and he had the best possible partner for what lay ahead. For the first time since Tori had disappeared, he felt something other than desperation.

He felt like Phoenix.

The drive to the North Cascades would take them through some of the most beautiful country in Washington State, but Marcus barely noticed the scenery. His mind was focused on the tactical challenges ahead, running through scenarios and contingencies with the methodical precision that had once made him one of the CIA's most effective operatives.

Sarah rode in the passenger seat, monitoring communications traffic and coordinating with resources that officially didn't exist. She'd brought more than just intelligence to Seattle – she'd brought the backing of people who understood that some threats required unofficial responses.

"Thermal imaging shows two heat signatures at the target location," she reported as they climbed into the mountains. "One stationary, probably Tori, and one mobile, probably Elena."

"No backup?"
"Not at the cabin itself. But there are at least three other vehicles positioned along the access road, and I'm picking up radio chatter that suggests a larger support team." Sarah adjusted her equipment. "Elena may be young, but she's not stupid. She's prepared for the possibility that you might not come alone."

"Good. That means she's taking this seriously."

"It also means she's more dangerous than we initially thought. This isn't just about revenge anymore – it's about proving herself to her father and his organization."

Marcus understood the implications. Elena wasn't just seeking justice for her brother's death – she was trying to establish her credentials as a worthy successor to Viktor's criminal empire. Killing Phoenix would be the kind of achievement that would cement her reputation and open doors throughout the international underworld.

"She's going to be disappointed," Marcus said.

"Let's make sure of that."

As they approached the final checkpoint before the target area, Sarah made one last equipment check. She would be providing overwatch from a position about half a mile from the cabin, close enough to provide support but far enough away to avoid detection. Marcus would go in alone, as Elena had demanded, but he wouldn't be as alone as she thought.

"Remember," Sarah said as they prepared to separate, "Elena wants to talk before she kills you. She needs to justify what she's doing, to make you understand why you deserve to die. Use that time to locate Tori and assess the tactical situation."

"And if talking doesn't work?"

"Then you do what Phoenix does best. You survive, and you make sure the people who threatened your family don't get a second chance."

Marcus checked his weapons one final time and started walking toward the cabin, knowing that the next few hours would determine whether he and Tori had a future together or whether they would both become casualties of a war that had started long before they met.

Behind him, Sarah melted into the forest like a ghost, taking up a position that would give her clear fields of fire on the cabin and its approaches. She was the best backup
he could ask for, but ultimately, this confrontation would come down to him and Elena, Phoenix and the daughter of the man whose son he'd killed in Prague.

The game was entering its final phase, and Marcus intended to win.

Chapter 7: Captive

The cabin where Elena had brought her was nothing like the luxury properties Tori was accustomed to showing. It was rustic and isolated, built from rough-hewn logs and situated in a small clearing surrounded by towering evergreens. Under different circumstances, she might have found it charming – the kind of mountain retreat that wealthy clients sometimes sought for weekend getaways. But with her hands zip-tied behind her back and Elena's gun never far from reach, the cabin felt more like a prison than a refuge.

Tori sat in a wooden chair near the stone fireplace, trying to process everything that had happened in the past twelve hours. The woman she'd known as a potential client had revealed herself to be something far more dangerous – someone with a personal vendetta against the man Tori had married. The accusations Elena had made about Marcus seemed impossible, but they explained so many things that had never quite made sense.

His reluctance to talk about his past. The way he sometimes seemed hyperaware of his surroundings, as if he were constantly scanning for threats. The occasional nightmare that would wake him in the middle of the night, leaving him tense and alert until dawn. The substantial savings account that had allowed him to start his development company without traditional financing.

"You're thinking about him," Elena said from across the room, where she was monitoring what appeared to be sophisticated communications equipment. "Wondering if what I told you could possibly be true."

"I'm thinking about how someone could be so consumed by hatred that they'd kidnap an innocent person," Tori replied, surprised by the steadiness of her own voice. Fear had given way to anger, and anger was something she could work with.

"Innocent." Elena laughed, but there was no humor in the sound. "Do you know what your husband was doing eight years ago while you were probably showing houses to nice suburban families?"
"Building his business. Learning about sustainable development and urban planning."

"He was in Prague, leading a team of CIA operatives in a raid on a warehouse complex. Their mission was to gather intelligence on an arms dealing operation and arrest the key players." Elena's voice took on a bitter edge. "But something went wrong. There was resistance, gunfire, and when the smoke cleared, my nineteen-year-old brother was dead."

Tori felt her heart clench at the pain in Elena's voice, even as her mind rejected the implications. "If your brother was involved with arms dealers—"

"My brother was a college student who worked part-time as a translator. He spoke six languages fluently, and he was trying to earn money for medical school." Elena turned away from her equipment to face Tori directly. "He was in that warehouse because he'd been hired to translate documents, not because he was a criminal."

"Then why didn't he surrender when the authorities arrived?"

"Because he was nineteen years old and terrified, and he made the mistake of running instead of putting his hands up." Elena's composure cracked slightly, revealing the grief that drove her. "Your husband shot him twice in the back as he tried to escape through a window."

The image Elena painted was devastating, and Tori found herself struggling to reconcile it with the gentle man she'd married. Marcus, who rescued spiders from the bathtub because he couldn't bear to kill them. Marcus, who cried during sad movies and brought her flowers for no reason other than that he'd seen them and thought of her.

"Even if that's true," Tori said carefully, "it doesn't justify this. Kidnapping me won't bring your brother back."

"No, but it will bring your husband here, and when he arrives, we'll have a conversation about justice and consequences." Elena checked her watch. "He has about six hours left to make his decision."

"What decision?"

"Whether he loves you enough to die for you. Whether Marcus Sterling is willing to let Phoenix be reborn one last time."

The name Phoenix meant nothing to Tori, but the way Elena said it suggested it was significant. Another piece of the puzzle that was her husband's hidden past, another secret that had been kept from her throughout their marriage.

"You keep talking about Phoenix. What does that mean?"

"It was his operational codename. Phoenix – the bird that rises from the ashes. Very poetic for a killer." Elena moved to the window and peered through the curtains at the forest beyond. "He was good at his job, I'll give him that. Very good at becoming someone new when his old identity was compromised."

"Like becoming Marcus Sterling?"

"Exactly like becoming Marcus Sterling. The CIA helped him create a new identity when he left the agency, complete with a background that would stand up to casual scrutiny. Real estate development was perfect – it explained his wealth, his connections, his ability to travel when necessary."

Tori felt as if the ground was shifting beneath her feet. Everything she thought she knew about her husband, about their life together, was being called into question. But even as doubt crept in, she found herself clinging to the moments that couldn't be fabricated. The way Marcus looked at her when he thought she wasn't watching. The tenderness in his touch when she was sick or upset. The absolute certainty in his voice when he told her he loved her.

"You're wrong about one thing," Tori said.

"What's that?"

"Marcus doesn't have to choose between loving me and being whoever he used to be. He can be both.

People aren't just one thing, Elena. They're complex, and they can change."

Elena's expression softened slightly, as if Tori's words had touched something vulnerable inside her. "I used to believe that. Before my brother died, I thought people could be redeemed, that they could move beyond their past mistakes." She turned back to her equipment. "But some actions can't be undone, and some debts can only be paid in blood."

"Is that what your father taught you?"
The question hit its mark, and Elena's face hardened. "My father taught me that the world is divided into predators and prey, and that the only way to avoid being prey is to become a predator yourself."

"And which one am I?"

"You're collateral damage. An innocent person caught up in something that started long before you met your husband." Elena's voice carried a note of genuine regret. "I'm sorry about that, Tori. I really am. Under different circumstances, I think we might have been friends."

"We still could be. It's not too late to stop this."

"Yes, it is. The moment your husband killed my

brother, it became too late." Elena checked her communications equipment again. "He's coming, by the way. My surveillance team picked up his vehicle about an hour ago. He's being very careful, very professional, but he's definitely coming."

Tori felt a mixture of relief and terror. Relief that Marcus was alive and trying to rescue her, terror at what might happen when he arrived. If Elena was right about his past, if he really had been a CIA operative, then he was walking into a trap designed specifically for someone with his skills and training.

"How many people are you planning to kill today?" Tori asked.

"As few as possible. Ideally, just your husband. But if he brings backup, if he tries to turn this into some kind of military operation, then more people will die." Elena's tone was matter-of-fact, as if she were discussing the weather. "The choice is his."

"And what about me? What happens to me after you've had your revenge?"

Elena was quiet for a long moment, and Tori could see her struggling with the question. "I haven't decided yet. You're not my enemy, but you're also a witness to what's about to happen."

"I could disappear. Leave Seattle, start over somewhere else. You'd never see me again."

"Could you? Could you really just walk away from the life you've built, from the man you love, and pretend none of this ever happened?" Elena shook her head. "No, I don't think you could. You'd go to the authorities, or you'd try to find some way to get revenge of your own."

"So you're planning to kill me too."

"I'm planning to do whatever is necessary to protect myself and complete my mission. If that means killing you, then yes, I'll kill you." Elena's voice was steady, but Tori could see the conflict in her eyes. "But I hope it doesn't come to that."

They sat in silence for several minutes, each lost in their own thoughts. Tori found herself studying Elena, trying to understand the woman who held her life in her hands. She was young, probably not much older than Tori had been when she'd first met Marcus. Beautiful, intelligent, and clearly well-educated. Under different circumstances, Elena might have been a successful businesswoman or academic, someone who used her talents to build rather than destroy.

"Can I ask you something?" Tori said.

"What?"

"What did you want to be when you were a little girl? Before all this happened, what were your dreams?"

The question seemed to catch Elena off guard, and for a moment, her carefully maintained composure slipped. "I wanted to be a doctor. Like my brother. We were going to open a clinic together, provide medical care to people who couldn't afford it."

"You still could. After this is over, you could go back to school, pursue that dream."

"No, I couldn't. I've done things, Tori. Things that can't be undone. I'm not the same person who wanted to save lives." Elena's voice was hollow. "That girl died in Prague along with my brother."

"People can change. You said it yourself – they can move beyond their past mistakes."

"Some people can. But not me. I've gone too far down this path to turn back now." Elena stood up and moved to the window again. "He's close. My perimeter team reports movement about two miles out."

Tori's heart began to race. Whatever was going to happen, it would happen soon. She thought about

Marcus, about the man she'd married and the life they'd built together. Whatever secrets he'd kept, whatever he might have done in his past, she knew with absolute certainty that he loved her. That love was real, even if everything else had been a carefully constructed lie.

"Elena," she said, "when Marcus gets here, when you have your confrontation, remember that revenge won't bring your brother back. It won't heal the pain you're carrying. It will just create more pain, more loss, more people who have to live with the consequences of violence."

"Maybe. But it will also ensure that the man who killed my brother pays for what he did."

"And what about the woman who loves him? What about the life we've built together? Does that count for nothing?"

Elena turned from the window, and Tori could see tears in her eyes. "It counts for everything. That's what makes this so hard. But it doesn't change what has to happen."

Outside, the sound of a vehicle engine grew closer, then stopped. Elena immediately became alert, checking her weapons and communications equipment with professional efficiency. The grieving sister was gone, replaced by the trained operative who had spent years planning this moment.

"He's here," Elena said, and Tori could hear both anticipation and dread in her voice.

Through the cabin's windows, Tori could see a figure moving through the trees – tall, familiar, moving with a careful precision that she'd never noticed before. It was Marcus, but somehow different. There was something in his posture, in the way he carried himself, that spoke of danger and capability.

"Remember," Elena called out, her voice carrying through the forest, "you come alone, or she dies."

"I'm alone," Marcus replied, his voice steady and calm. "Let me see her."

Elena gestured for Tori to stand and move to the window where Marcus could see her. Their eyes met across the clearing, and Tori saw something in his expression that she'd never seen before – a cold, calculating assessment that was completely at odds with the gentle man she'd married.

"I'm okay," she called out, hoping her

voice would carry. "I'm not hurt." "Good,"

Marcus replied. "Elena, let's talk. You and

me. Leave Tori out of this."

"She's already in it. She became part of it the moment she married you." Elena stepped into view, her gun trained on Tori. "Come closer, Phoenix. Let's finish what we started in Prague."

As Marcus began walking toward the cabin, Tori realized that she was about to witness the collision of two worlds – the life she'd known and the life her husband had left behind. Whatever happened in the next few minutes would determine whether they had a future together or whether the past would finally claim them both.

The final act was about to begin.

Chapter 8: Hidden Skills

Marcus moved through the forest with a fluidity that came from years of training and experience, every sense alert to potential threats. The transformation from Marcus Sterling to Phoenix hadn't been gradual –

it had been instantaneous, triggered by the sight of Tori in danger and the familiar weight of weapons in his hands. The businessman who had left Seattle that morning was gone, replaced by the operative who had once been feared throughout the international intelligence community.

He could feel Elena watching him from the cabin, probably through a scope or binoculars. She would be assessing his approach, looking for signs of backup or deception. But Marcus had been doing this longer than she'd been alive, and he knew how to give an opponent exactly what they expected to see while preparing for something entirely different.

His earpiece crackled with Sarah's voice, transmitted on a frequency that Elena's equipment wouldn't be monitoring. "I count three overwatch positions along your route. Professional placement, good fields of fire. This girl knows what she's doing."

"Acknowledged," Marcus subvocalized, the words barely audible even to himself. "Tori's status?"

"Alive and mobile. I can see her through the cabin's front window. Elena's keeping her close, using her as a human shield." Sarah's voice was clinical, professional. "Marcus, the thermal imaging shows at least two other heat signatures in the cabin. Elena's not alone in there."

The information didn't surprise Marcus, but it complicated the tactical situation. Elena had claimed to want a personal confrontation, but she was smart enough to have backup. The question was whether her associates were there to help her kill him or to ensure she didn't lose her nerve at the crucial moment.

"Rules of engagement?" Sarah asked.

"Minimize casualties, but protect Tori at all costs. If it comes down to a choice between Elena's people and my wife, there is no choice."

"Understood."

Marcus reached the edge of the clearing and paused, using the moment to assess the tactical situation. The cabin was well-positioned, with clear sight lines in all directions and limited approaches that could be easily defended. Elena had chosen her ground carefully, but she'd also made some mistakes. The windows were large and unprotected, offering good visibility but also creating vulnerabilities. The single door was a potential bottleneck, and the wooden construction wouldn't stop high-powered rifle rounds.

"Phoenix," Elena called out from inside the cabin. "I can see you thinking. Calculating angles, assessing threats, planning your approach. It's exactly what I expected from someone with your reputation."

"My reputation is probably exaggerated," Marcus replied, stepping into the clearing with his hands visible but ready to move. "I was just a government employee doing a job."

"A job that included killing my brother."

"A job that included stopping arms dealers from selling weapons to terrorists. Your brother was in the wrong place at the wrong time, and I'm sorry for that. But I won't apologize for doing what was necessary to protect innocent lives."

Elena appeared in the cabin's doorway, her gun trained on Marcus while keeping Tori within reach. Even from a distance, Marcus could see the resemblance to Viktor Kozlov – the same dark eyes, the same stubborn set to her jaw. But where Viktor was calculating and cold, Elena burned with the kind of righteous anger that made people dangerous.
"Innocent lives," she repeated. "Like my brother's life? He was innocent, Phoenix. He was a student, a translator, someone who had never hurt anyone in his

entire life."

"I know. And I've carried that weight for eight years." Marcus took another step closer, his hands still visible but his body positioned to move in any direction. "But killing me won't bring him back, Elena. It will just create more grief, more loss, more people who have to live with the consequences of violence."

"Maybe. But it will also ensure that you pay for what you did."

Marcus could see Tori through the window, her face pale but determined. She was watching the exchange with the kind of focused attention that suggested she was looking for an opportunity to help. It was exactly what he would have expected from her – even in the face of mortal danger, she was thinking tactically, trying to find a way to influence the outcome.

"What do you want from me, Elena? An apology? An admission of guilt? My life?" Marcus stopped about twenty feet from the cabin, close enough to talk normally but far enough away to have room to maneuver. "Tell me what it will take to end this."

"I want you to understand what you took from my family. I want you to feel the same loss, the same helplessness, that we felt when we learned Alexei was dead." Elena's voice was steady, but Marcus could hear the emotion underneath. "I want you to watch the woman you love die, and then I want to kill you slowly."

"That's not going to happen."

"No? You're outnumbered, outgunned, and in the middle of nowhere. My people have been watching you since you left Seattle, and they're in position to kill you the moment I give the word." Elena's confidence was genuine, but Marcus could also hear the uncertainty beneath it. "You're not the legendary Phoenix anymore. You're just a middle-aged businessman who's been playing house for seven years."

"You might be right," Marcus said, and then he moved.

The transformation was instantaneous and complete. One moment he was standing in the clearing like a concerned husband trying to negotiate for his wife's life, and the next he was a blur of motion, diving toward the tree line as gunfire erupted from multiple positions around the cabin.

Elena's overwatch team had been well-positioned, but they'd made the mistake of assuming that Marcus would behave like a civilian. Instead, he moved like the professional he'd once been, using the terrain and his knowledge of their positions to stay ahead of their targeting solutions.

Sarah's voice crackled in his earpiece: "Three shooters, positions marked. I'm engaging the one on your left flank."

The sound of her sniper rifle was sharp and final, and Marcus knew that Elena's team was now down to two. He rolled behind a fallen log as bullets chewed up the ground where he'd been standing, then came up with his own weapon ready.

The second shooter was in a tree about fifty yards to his right, using the elevation to maintain visual contact despite the forest cover. Marcus put two rounds center mass, and the man fell from his perch like a broken doll.

"One left," Sarah reported. "He's moving to flank you from the north."

Marcus was already moving, using his knowledge of the terrain to anticipate the remaining shooter's approach. The man was good – probably ex-military or private security – but he was also predictable. He would try to get behind Marcus, to catch him in a crossfire with Elena's position at the cabin.

Instead, Marcus circled wide and came up behind him, moving through the forest with the silent efficiency that had made him legendary among his peers. The shooter never saw him coming.

"Clear," Marcus reported, and then he focused his attention on the cabin where Elena held his wife.

"Impressive," Elena called out, her voice carrying clearly through the forest. "But it doesn't change anything. I still have Tori, and I still have enough firepower to kill both of you if you try anything heroic."

"Let her go, Elena. This is between you and me."

"No, it's between you and the consequences of your actions. Tori is part of those consequences now." Elena's voice was harder now, the grief and anger crystallizing into something more dangerous. "Come into the cabin, Phoenix. Come face the family you destroyed."

Marcus moved closer to the cabin, using the trees for cover while he assessed the situation. Through the windows, he could see Elena holding Tori at gunpoint, but he could also see something else – Tori was positioned near a window, and she was making subtle gestures with her hands. She was trying to communicate something, using a simple code that they'd developed for situations where they needed to coordinate without speaking.

Two more people inside. Armed. Watching the back door.

Marcus smiled grimly. Even in the middle of a life-or-death situation, Tori was thinking like a partner, gathering intelligence and finding ways to help. It was one of the reasons he'd fallen in love with her – her ability to stay calm under pressure and find solutions when other people would panic.

"I'm coming in," Marcus called out. "But I want to see Tori walk out first. Proof of good faith."

"The only proof you'll get is that she's still breathing. Come inside, hands visible, weapons on the ground. Any tricks, and she dies."

Marcus considered his options. The direct approach was exactly what Elena expected, but it was also the most dangerous. She had backup inside the cabin, good defensive positions, and a hostage she was willing to kill. But she also had something that could be used against her – her need to confront him personally, to make him understand why she was doing this.

"Sarah," he subvocalized, "I'm going in. Be ready to provide support if this goes sideways."

"Copy that. I'll maintain overwatch and wait for your signal."

Marcus emerged from the tree line with his hands visible, his primary weapon on the ground behind him. But he still had the compact pistol tucked into his waistband, hidden beneath his jacket, and he had something more valuable than any weapon – the knowledge that Elena needed him alive long enough to have her confrontation.

"That's far enough," Elena said as he approached the cabin door. "Turn around, let me see that you're not carrying any surprises."

Marcus complied, turning slowly with his arms extended. Elena was being thorough, but she was also focused on him rather than on potential threats from other
directions. It was a mistake that Sarah could exploit if necessary.

"Now come inside. Slowly. Keep your hands where I can see them."

Marcus pushed open the cabin door and stepped inside, immediately assessing the tactical situation. Elena was positioned near the fireplace with Tori beside her, the gun pressed against his wife's temple. Two other men were positioned near the back door, both armed with assault rifles and looking nervous. They were professionals, but they were also clearly uncomfortable with the situation.

"Hello, Phoenix," Elena said, her voice carrying a mixture of triumph and sadness. "Welcome to the reckoning."

Marcus looked at Tori, seeing the fear in her eyes but also the determination. She was ready to act if an opportunity presented itself, ready to trust him to get them both out of this alive.

"Hello, Elena," he replied. "I think it's time we had that conversation."

Chapter 9: Phoenix Rising

Prague, Czech Republic – Eight Years Earlier

The warehouse district on the outskirts of Prague was a maze of abandoned buildings and forgotten industrial complexes, the kind of place where illegal transactions could occur without attracting unwanted attention. Phoenix moved through the shadows with practiced ease, his team spread out in a coordinated pattern that would allow them to converge on the target building from multiple directions.

"Overwatch in position," Sarah's voice crackled through his earpiece. She was stationed on a rooftop three blocks away, providing surveillance and coordination for the operation.

"Copy that," Phoenix replied, his voice barely above a whisper. "Alpha team, report." "Alpha in position, south entrance secured."

"Bravo team?"

"Bravo ready, north entrance covered."
Phoenix checked his watch. They had been tracking Viktor Kozlov's arms dealing operation for six months, gathering intelligence and building a case that would shut down one of Eastern Europe's most dangerous weapons trafficking networks. Tonight was the culmination of that work – a coordinated raid designed to capture Viktor, seize his weapons cache, and dismantle his organization.

"Remember, we want Viktor alive if possible," Phoenix said. "But if anyone starts shooting, protect yourselves and complete the mission."

The warehouse was larger than it appeared from the outside, with multiple levels and a complex layout that provided numerous hiding places and escape routes. Intelligence suggested that Viktor was using the building as both a storage facility and a meeting place, conducting business with buyers from across the globe.

Phoenix approached the main entrance, noting the sophisticated security measures that Viktor had installed. Motion sensors, cameras, and what appeared to be pressure plates beneath the flooring. The man was paranoid, but he had good reason to be – his business had made him enemies throughout the intelligence community.

"Thermal imaging shows at least twelve heat signatures inside," Sarah reported. "Most are clustered in the main warehouse area, but there are two or three moving around the perimeter."

"Acknowledged. Beginning entry."

Phoenix disabled the security system with equipment

that officially didn't exist, then slipped inside the warehouse like a ghost. The interior was dimly lit, with crates and shipping containers creating a labyrinth of hiding places. He could hear voices speaking in Russian and what sounded like Arabic, confirming that a major transaction was in progress.

Moving closer to the voices, Phoenix positioned himself behind a stack of wooden crates and activated his recording equipment. The intelligence they gathered tonight would be used to identify Viktor's buyers and suppliers, potentially disrupting weapons trafficking operations across multiple continents.

"Phoenix, we have a problem," Sarah's voice was urgent. "Local police are responding to reports of suspicious activity. You have maybe ten minutes before they arrive."

The timeline had just accelerated dramatically. Phoenix signaled his teams to move in, knowing that they needed to complete the operation before the local authorities complicated the situation.

"Go, go, go!"

The warehouse erupted in controlled chaos as

Phoenix's team moved in from multiple directions. Shouts in several languages filled the air as Viktor's people realized they were under attack. Phoenix moved through the maze of containers with deadly efficiency, neutralizing threats and securing evidence.

He found Viktor in a makeshift office area, frantically trying to destroy documents while his bodyguards prepared to make a last stand. The arms dealer was older than his photographs suggested, with gray hair and the kind of hard eyes that came from a lifetime of violence.

"Viktor Kozlov, you're under arrest," Phoenix announced, his weapon trained on the man who had been responsible for arming terrorists and insurgents across three continents.

"Phoenix," Viktor said, his English accented but clear. "I wondered when you would find me."

"It was only a matter of time. Your operation is finished, Viktor. Your people are in custody, your weapons are seized, and your network is blown."

"Perhaps. But you cannot arrest an idea, and you cannot kill a cause. Others will take my place."

"Maybe. But they'll have to start from scratch, and that will save lives."

The sound of gunfire from another part of the warehouse interrupted their conversation. Phoenix's earpiece crackled with reports from his team – they had encountered more resistance than expected, and the situation was deteriorating rapidly.

"Phoenix, we have civilians in the building," Alpha team reported. "Looks like Viktor was using local kids as runners and translators. They're caught in the crossfire."

The information changed everything. Phoenix had been prepared for a straightforward arrest operation, but the presence of civilians meant that every decision could result in innocent casualties.

"Get them out of there," Phoenix ordered. "Priority one is civilian safety."
"Copy that. We're moving to evacuate."

Phoenix kept his weapon trained on Viktor while coordinating the evacuation through his earpiece. The arms dealer watched with what might have been amusement, as if he understood that the presence of civilians had shifted the tactical balance in his favor.

"You see?" Viktor said. "This is why you will never truly defeat us. You care too much about innocent lives, and we are willing to sacrifice anyone to achieve our goals."

"That's what makes us different from you."

"That's what makes you weak."

The sound of running footsteps echoed through the warehouse, and Phoenix could hear his team calling out in English and Czech, trying to identify civilians and separate them from Viktor's people. It was exactly the kind of chaotic situation that led to tragic mistakes.

"Phoenix, we have a runner!" Bravo team reported. "Young male, heading for the east exit. He's not responding to commands to stop."

Through his earpiece, Phoenix could hear the tension in his team member's voice. In the darkness and confusion, it was impossible to tell whether the runner was a civilian trying to escape or one of Viktor's people attempting to flee with evidence or weapons.

"Do not engage unless you're certain of the threat," Phoenix ordered. "Repeat, do not engage unless you're certain."

But even as he spoke, Phoenix knew that his team was operating under extreme stress, with split-second decisions that could mean the difference between life and death. In situations like this, training took over, and training said that anyone who ran from law enforcement was potentially hostile.

The sound of gunfire from the east side of the building was sharp and final. Two shots, fired in rapid succession.

"Target down," Bravo team reported. "Runner is neutralized."

"Status of the target?"

There was a pause, and Phoenix could hear the tension in the silence. "Phoenix, we have a problem. The runner was a civilian. Young male, maybe nineteen or twenty. He was carrying translation documents, not weapons."

The words hit Phoenix like a physical blow. An innocent person was dead because of decisions he had made, because of an operation he had planned and executed. The fact that it had been a mistake, that his team member had acted according to training and protocol, didn't change the fundamental reality.

"Secure the scene and continue the evacuation," Phoenix said, his voice steady despite the turmoil in his mind. "We'll deal with the aftermath later."

Viktor was watching him with something that might have been sympathy. "His name was Alexei," the arms dealer said quietly. "He was my son."

The revelation was like a knife to the heart. Phoenix stared at Viktor, seeing the grief and rage that the older man was struggling to contain. The civilian who had died wasn't just an innocent bystander – he was Viktor's child, caught up in his father's criminal activities but not truly part of them.

"I'm sorry," Phoenix said, and meant it.

"Sorry doesn't bring him back. Sorry doesn't undo what you've done." Viktor's voice was hollow, empty of everything except pain. "You came here to destroy my operation, and you succeeded. But you also destroyed my family."

"He shouldn't have been here, Viktor. You shouldn't have put him in danger."

"He was trying to earn money for medical school. He wanted to be a doctor, to save lives instead of taking them." Viktor's composure finally cracked, and Phoenix could see the father beneath the criminal. "He was everything good that I could never be, and now he's dead because of your war against me."

Phoenix felt the weight of command, the burden of decisions that had consequences far beyond their intended scope. He had come to Prague to stop a weapons dealer, and he had succeeded. But he had also created a tragedy that would haunt everyone involved for the rest of their lives.

"Sir, we need to move," Alpha team reported. "Local police are two minutes out, and we need to be gone before they arrive."

Phoenix looked at Viktor one last time, seeing not just a criminal but a father who had lost his child. "This doesn't have to define you, Viktor. You can choose to end the cycle of violence."
"Can I? Can you?" Viktor's eyes were hard again, the grief transforming into something more dangerous. "You've taken everything from me, Phoenix. My son, my business, my reason for living. What do you think I'll choose to do with the rest of my life?"

Phoenix didn't answer, because he already knew. Viktor would choose revenge, and that choice would eventually lead to this moment in a cabin in the Cascade Mountains, with Elena holding a gun to Tori's head.

Present Day – Cascade Mountains

"You remember him, don't you?" Elena said, watching Phoenix's face as the memories played out. "My brother. The boy you killed in Prague."

"I remember," Phoenix replied, his voice steady despite the emotions churning inside him. "I remember everything about that night."

"Do you remember what he looked like when they brought his body home? Do you remember the funeral, the way my mother cried, the way my father changed?" Elena's voice was thick with pain. "Do you remember how it felt to destroy a family?"

"I remember that your brother was in the wrong place at the wrong time, and I'm sorry for that. But I also remember that your father was selling weapons to terrorists, and that those weapons were being used to kill innocent people."

"Innocent people like Alexei?"

"Yes. Like Alexei." Phoenix took a step closer, ignoring

the gun that Elena kept trained on Tori. "Your brother's death was a tragedy, Elena. But it was also an accident, a consequence of your father's choices, not mine."

"You pulled the trigger."

"My team member pulled the trigger, acting on training and protocol in a chaotic situation. If you want to blame someone for Alexei's death, blame the man who put him in that warehouse in the first place."

Elena's face contorted with rage. "Don't you dare blame my father for your actions!"

"I'm not blaming him for my actions. I'm blaming him for his. Viktor chose to involve his son in his criminal activities. Viktor chose to use children as runners and translators. Viktor chose to put Alexei in danger." Phoenix's voice was calm, but there was steel underneath. "I came to Prague to stop a weapons dealer. Your father made it personal by involving his family."

"He was trying to give Alexei a better life!"

"By exposing him to violence and criminality? By making him complicit in arms dealing?" Phoenix shook his head. "Your father loved Alexei, I don't doubt that.

But love isn't enough if it leads to destructive choices."

Tori watched the exchange with growing understanding. She could see the pain in Elena's eyes, the grief that had been twisted into hatred over eight years of planning and preparation. But she could also see the truth in Marcus's words, the complexity of a situation that had no clear heroes or villains.

"Elena," Tori said softly, "I know you loved your brother. I can see it in everything you do, everything you say. But killing Marcus won't bring Alexei back. It will just create more grief, more loss, more families torn apart by violence."

"She's right," one of Elena's associates said from his position near the back door. "This has gone far enough. We came here to send a message, not to start a war."

Elena spun around, her gun now pointed at her own team member. "We came here to get justice for Alexei!"

"We came here because Viktor promised us a fortune to kill Phoenix," the man replied. "But I didn't sign up to murder innocent women or to die in some personal vendetta that should have ended years ago."

The admission hung in the air like a revelation. Elena's operation wasn't just about revenge – it was about money, about proving herself to her father's organization, about establishing her credentials in the criminal underworld.

"You're just like him," Phoenix said, understanding flooding through him. "You're just like Viktor. You've turned your brother's death into a business opportunity."

"No!" Elena's voice was anguished. "This is about justice! This is about making you pay for what you did!"

"This is about proving to your father that you're worthy of inheriting his empire. Alexei's death is just the excuse you're using to justify becoming everything he would have hated."

Elena's composure finally shattered completely. She turned the gun back toward Phoenix, her finger tightening on the trigger. "You don't know anything about my brother!"

"I know he wanted to be a doctor. I know he wanted to save lives. I know he would be horrified by what you've become in his name."

The words hit their target, and Elena's face crumpled with grief and rage. But before she could pull the trigger, Tori acted.

With a speed that surprised everyone in the room, Tori threw herself sideways, breaking Elena's grip and creating the opening that Phoenix had been waiting for. His hidden pistol was in his hand before Elena could react, and the two men by the back door found themselves facing Sarah's sniper rifle through the window.

"It's over, Elena," Phoenix said, his weapon trained on the woman who had torn his life apart. "Put the gun down."

Elena looked around the room, seeing her operation collapsing and her associates surrendering. The grief and rage that had sustained her for eight years was finally giving way to the reality of what she had become.

"It's not over," she said, but her voice lacked conviction. "It will never be over."

"It is if you choose to make it over. You can honor your brother's memory by choosing to heal instead of destroy, by choosing to build instead of tear down."

Elena stared at him for a long moment, and Phoenix could see the war being fought behind her eyes. The daughter who had loved her brother was battling with the criminal who had been shaped by years of hatred and planning.

Finally, slowly, she lowered her weapon.

"What happens now?" she asked.

"Now," Phoenix said, "we figure out how to end this cycle of violence once and for all."

Chapter 10: Psychological Warfare

The tension in the cabin was palpable, like the moment before a thunderstorm when the air itself seems to vibrate with potential energy. Elena had lowered her weapon,
but she hadn't surrendered it, and Phoenix could see the conflict still raging behind her eyes. Her associates remained frozen in position, caught between their orders and their survival instincts.

"Sarah," Phoenix subvocalized, "status report."

"I have clear shots on both targets by the back door. Elena is partially blocked by Tori's position, but I can take her if necessary." Sarah's voice was calm and professional. "What are your intentions?"

"Stand by. I think we can resolve this without more bloodshed."

Phoenix kept his weapon trained on Elena while addressing her directly. "You said this was about justice for your brother. But justice isn't the same thing as revenge, Elena. Justice is about preventing future tragedies, not perpetuating past ones."

"Don't lecture me about justice," Elena replied, but her voice lacked the venom it had carried earlier. "You don't know what it's like to lose family."

"Actually, I do." Phoenix's voice was quiet, carrying a weight that made everyone in the room pay attention. "I lost my parents when I was twelve. Car accident, drunk driver. I spent six years in foster care, moving from home to home, never staying anywhere long enough to form real connections."

Tori stared at her husband, hearing details about his past that he'd never shared with her. She'd known he was an orphan, but he'd never talked about the specifics, never revealed the pain that had shaped his early years.

"The CIA recruited me when I was eighteen," Phoenix continued. "They offered me purpose, belonging, a chance to make a difference in the world. For fifteen years, I believed that what I was doing mattered, that the sacrifices were worth it."

"And now?" Elena asked.

"Now I know that the most important thing in life isn't the mission or the cause. It's the people you choose to love and protect." Phoenix glanced at Tori, his expression softening for just a moment. "Your brother understood that. He was working to become a doctor, to save lives, to build something positive in the world."

"He was trying to earn money for medical school," Elena said, her voice breaking slightly. "He took the translation job because we needed the money, because our father's business had made us targets and we couldn't live normal lives."

"Then honor his memory by choosing a different path. Break the cycle of violence that destroyed your family."

Elena looked around the cabin, seeing her operation

falling apart and her carefully laid plans crumbling. "It's not that simple. You don't understand the forces at work here, the people who are depending on me to succeed."

"Viktor."

"Among others. My father's organization has invested heavily in this operation. They expect results, and they don't accept failure gracefully."

Phoenix understood the implications. Elena wasn't just seeking personal revenge – she was trapped in a web of criminal obligations that would follow her for the rest of her life if she didn't complete her mission.

"What did Viktor promise them?" Phoenix asked.

"Your death, obviously. But also intelligence about other former CIA operatives, information that could be used to target them and their families." Elena's voice was hollow. "This was supposed to be the beginning of a larger campaign of revenge against everyone who was involved in Prague."

The revelation sent a chill through Phoenix. If Viktor was planning to target other former operatives, then dozens of innocent families could be at risk. The threat extended far beyond his own situation with Tori.

"How many names are on Viktor's list?"

"Fifteen. Maybe twenty. Everyone who was involved in the Prague operation, plus their handlers and support personnel." Elena met his eyes. "Your friend Sarah is on the list. So is Detective Morrison, once Viktor's people identified him as someone you trust."

Phoenix felt a surge of cold rage. Viktor wasn't just seeking revenge against him – he was planning to destroy everyone who had ever been connected to the operation that had killed his son. It was the kind of comprehensive vengeance that could only come from years of careful planning and unlimited resources.

"Where is Viktor now?" Phoenix asked.

"Safe. Protected. Surrounded by people who would die to keep him alive." Elena's smile was bitter. "Did you think he would expose himself by coming here personally?
He's learned from his mistakes."

"But you haven't learned from his."

The words hit their mark, and Elena's composure cracked again. "What's that supposed to mean?"

"It means you're repeating the same pattern that got your brother killed. You're putting yourself in danger for Viktor's agenda, just like Alexei put himself in danger for Viktor's business." Phoenix took a step closer. "The only difference is that this time, Viktor is using grief and guilt to manipulate you instead of money and opportunity."

"That's not true."

"Isn't it? Think about it, Elena. When did Viktor first suggest that you should seek revenge against me? Was it immediately after Alexei's death, when you were grieving and vulnerable? Or was it later, after you'd had time to process the loss and move forward with your life?"

Elena's silence was answer enough. Phoenix could see the realization dawning in her eyes, the understanding that she had been manipulated just as thoroughly as her brother had been.

"He waited," Phoenix continued. "He let you grieve, let you heal, and then he reopened the wound when it served his purposes. He turned your love for your brother into a weapon against his enemies."

"Stop." Elena's voice was barely above a whisper.

"He's using you, Elena. Just like he used Alexei. The only difference is that this time, he's using your need for justice instead of your need for money."

"Stop!" Elena raised her weapon again, but her hands were shaking. "You don't know what you're talking about!"

"I know that your brother would be ashamed of what you've become in his name. I know that he would want you to choose healing over hatred, building over destroying." Phoenix's voice was gentle but relentless. "I know that the best way to honor his memory is to become the doctor he wanted to be, to save lives instead of taking them."

Elena's face was streaked with tears, and Phoenix could see the war being fought in her soul. The grief and rage that had sustained her for eight years were finally being challenged by the love and hope that her brother had represented.

"It's too late," she said. "I've done things. Terrible things. I can't go back."

"It's never too late to choose a different path. But you have to choose it, Elena. No one can make that choice for you."

Tori watched the exchange with growing understanding of the man she had married. This was Marcus at his core – not the businessman who built sustainable housing, not the husband who brought her flowers, but the person who could see past surface conflicts to the deeper human truths underneath. He was trying to save Elena not just from her own actions, but from the cycle of violence that had already claimed her brother.

"Elena," Tori said softly, "I know what it's like to love someone so much that you'd do anything to protect them. That's how I feel about Marcus, and I can see that's how you felt about your brother."

Elena turned to look at her, and Tori could see the pain and confusion in the younger woman's eyes.

"But love isn't about revenge," Tori continued. "It's about honoring the best parts of the person you've lost. If your brother wanted to be a doctor, if he wanted to save lives, then the best way to honor him is to save lives too. Starting with your own."

"I don't know how," Elena whispered.

"You start by putting down the gun," Phoenix said. "You start by choosing to trust that there's a better way forward than the path Viktor has set you on."

Elena stared at the weapon in her hands as if seeing it for the first time. Slowly, reluctantly, she set it down on the table beside her.

"What happens now?" she asked.

"Now we figure out how to keep you alive long enough to make different choices," Phoenix replied. "Because if Viktor's people realize you've failed, they'll kill you just as quickly as they'd kill me."

"He's right," one of Elena's associates said from his position by the back door. "Viktor doesn't tolerate failure, and he doesn't leave loose ends. If we don't complete this mission, we're all dead."

Phoenix looked at the two men, seeing the fear in their eyes. They were professionals, but they were also trapped in the same web of criminal obligations that held Elena. Their survival depended on completing a mission that had already gone sideways.

"What if we give Viktor what he wants?" Phoenix said.

"What do you mean?" Elena asked.

"What if we make him think the mission succeeded? What if Phoenix dies in this cabin, but Marcus

Sterling walks away?"

Sarah's voice crackled in his earpiece: "Marcus, what are you thinking?"

Phoenix touched his earpiece, signaling Sarah to maintain radio silence while he worked through the tactical problem. Viktor wanted revenge against Phoenix, but he'd never met Marcus Sterling. If they could stage Phoenix's death convincingly enough, it might buy them the time and space needed to dismantle Viktor's operation permanently.

"I'm thinking we fake my death," Phoenix said aloud, knowing that Sarah would hear him through the open channel. "Elena reports back to Viktor that the mission was successful, Phoenix is dead, and she's ready for the next phase of his revenge campaign."

"That's insane," Elena said. "Viktor isn't stupid. He'll want proof, verification, evidence that you're really dead."

"Then we'll give him evidence. Sarah has the technical resources to create whatever documentation Viktor needs to see." Phoenix looked at Elena directly. "But it only works if you're willing to play along, to pretend that you succeeded while actually working to bring down your father's organization from the inside."

Elena stared at him, and Phoenix could see her mind working through the implications. It was a dangerous game, one that would require her to deceive some of the most paranoid and violent people in the world. But it was also her only chance to escape the cycle of violence that had already claimed her brother.

"Why would you trust me?" she asked. "After everything I've done, why would you give me a chance to betray you again?"

"Because I think your brother was right about you. I think underneath all the anger and grief, you're someone who wants to heal the world instead of hurting it." Phoenix's voice was steady, certain. "And because the alternative is that we all die here today, and Viktor wins."

Elena looked around the cabin one more time, seeing the faces of people whose lives hung in the balance of her decision. Her associates, who had followed her into this operation. Tori, who had been caught up in something that had nothing to do with her. Phoenix, who was offering her a chance at redemption despite everything she had done.

"If I do this," she said slowly, "if I help you bring down

Viktor's organization, what happens to me afterward?"

"That depends on what you choose to do with your freedom," Phoenix replied. "But I know someone who might be able to help you disappear, to start over with a new identity and a clean slate."

"Like you did when you became Marcus Sterling?"

"Like I did when I became Marcus Sterling."

Elena closed her eyes, and Phoenix could see her making the most important decision of her life. When she opened them again, there was something different in her expression – not the cold determination of a killer, but the uncertain hope of someone choosing to trust in the possibility of redemption.

"Okay," she said. "Let's fake your death and bring down my father's empire."

Phoenix smiled, feeling a weight lift from his shoulders. The game was changing, the rules were shifting, and for the first time since Tori had been taken, he felt like they might actually win.

But first, they had to convince Viktor Kozlov that Phoenix was dead. And that would require the performance of their lives.

Chapter 11: Following the Trail

The plan to fake Phoenix's death required meticulous attention to detail and perfect timing. Sarah had withdrawn to her overwatch position to coordinate the technical aspects of the deception, while Phoenix worked with Elena and her associates to stage a convincing crime scene.

"Viktor will want photographic evidence," Elena explained as they arranged the cabin to look like the site of a violent confrontation. "He'll also want confirmation from multiple sources that you're actually dead."

"What kind of confirmation?" Phoenix asked, helping to overturn furniture and create the appearance of a struggle.

"Medical examiner's report, police statements, maybe even news coverage if the story is big enough." Elena paused in her work. "He's paranoid, but he's also thorough. He won't accept this unless it looks completely authentic."

Tori watched the preparations with a mixture of fascination and horror. Her husband was planning his own fake death with the same methodical precision he brought to his construction projects, treating it like just another problem to be solved through careful planning and execution.

"What about me?" she asked. "What's my role in this?"

"You're the grieving widow," Phoenix replied. "The innocent victim who witnessed her husband's murder and barely escaped with her life. Your testimony will be crucial to selling the story."

"I don't know if I can do that. I'm not an actress, Marcus. I don't know how to lie convincingly about something this important."

Phoenix stopped what he was doing and moved to her side, taking her hands in his. "You won't be lying about the important parts. You'll be telling the truth about being kidnapped, about being held at gunpoint, about fearing for your life. The only lie will be about how it ended."

"But what if I say something wrong? What if I give away the deception?"

"You won't. You're stronger than you know, Tori. You've already proven that by surviving this ordeal and helping us find a way forward." Phoenix's voice was gentle but confident. "Besides, the best lies are mostly truth. We're just changing the ending."

Sarah's voice crackled through Phoenix's earpiece: "I've got the technical side covered. Fake medical records, falsified police reports, even a staged crime scene photo that will pass casual inspection. But we need to move fast. Viktor's people will be expecting regular check-ins from Elena's team."

"How long do we have?" Phoenix asked.

"Maybe six hours before Viktor starts getting suspicious. After that, he'll send backup to investigate, and our window of opportunity closes."

Phoenix looked around the cabin, assessing what still needed to be done. They had created the appearance of a violent struggle, complete with bullet holes in the walls and blood stains on the floor. Sarah had provided the blood – a mixture of pig's blood and synthetic plasma that would fool forensic analysis unless someone looked very closely.

"Elena, I need you to call Viktor and give him a preliminary report," Phoenix said. "Tell him the mission is proceeding as planned, but don't give him details yet. We need to buy more time to set up the deception properly."

Elena nodded and pulled out a secure satellite phone. Phoenix could hear her side of the conversation as she spoke to her father in rapid Russian, her voice carrying the right mixture of confidence and caution.

"He's pleased but impatient," Elena reported after ending the call. "He wants a full report within four hours, including photographic evidence and confirmation that you're dead."

"We'll have it," Phoenix said. "Sarah, what's the status on our exit strategy?"

"I've got a helicopter standing by about ten miles from your location. Medical evacuation service, completely legitimate, with a pilot who doesn't ask questions about unusual passengers." Sarah's voice was crisp and professional. "Once we stage your death, we can extract you and Tori without leaving any traces for Viktor's people to follow."

"What about Elena and her team?"

"They'll need to return to Viktor and maintain their covers until we can move against his organization. It's dangerous, but it's the only way to get close enough to take him down permanently."

Phoenix looked at Elena, seeing the fear in her eyes despite her outward composure. She was agreeing to walk back into the lion's den, to deceive some of the most dangerous people in the world while secretly working to destroy them.

"Are you sure you can do this?" he asked.

"I have to. It's the only way to honor my brother's memory and break free from my father's influence." Elena's voice was steady, but Phoenix could hear the uncertainty underneath. "Besides, I've been preparing for this my entire life. I know Viktor's organization better than anyone except Viktor himself."

"That's what makes you valuable. But it's also what makes you dangerous to them if they suspect betrayal."

"I know the risks. But I also know that this is my only chance to choose a different path."

As they continued preparing the scene, Phoenix found himself studying Elena more closely. There was something familiar about her features, something that nagged at the edge of his memory. The shape of her eyes, the set of her jaw, the way she moved when she thought no one was watching.

"Elena," he said, "can I ask you something personal?"

"What?"

"What was your mother's name?"

The question seemed to catch Elena off guard. "Why do you want to know?"

"Just curious. You mentioned that you've been using her maiden name instead of Kozlov."

"Vasquez. Maria Vasquez." Elena's expression was guarded. "She died when I was sixteen. Cancer."

The name hit Phoenix like a physical blow. Maria Vasquez. He remembered her now – a beautiful woman with dark eyes and a quick smile, someone he'd met during his early years with the CIA. They'd had a brief relationship, intense but ultimately doomed by the demands of his career and the dangers of his work.

"When were you born, Elena?" Phoenix

asked, his voice carefully controlled.

"March 15th, 1995. Why?"

Phoenix did the math quickly, his mind racing through the implications. March 1995 would mean Elena had been conceived in June 1994, during the time when he'd been involved with Maria. The timing was right, the physical resemblance was there, and Maria had disappeared from his life without explanation just before he'd been deployed on a long-term assignment in Eastern Europe.

"Phoenix, what's wrong?" Sarah's voice crackled through his earpiece. "Your vitals just spiked."

Phoenix touched his earpiece, signaling Sarah to maintain radio silence while he processed this revelation. If Elena was his daughter, if Maria had been pregnant when she'd left him, then everything about this situation became infinitely more complicated.

"Elena," he said slowly, "did your mother ever mention working with American intelligence services?"

"She was a translator for various government agencies. Why are you asking these questions?"

"Because I think I knew your mother. I think we worked together, briefly, about twenty nine years ago."

Elena stared at him, and Phoenix could see understanding beginning to dawn in her eyes. The same eyes that looked back at him from the mirror every morning, the same stubborn determination that had driven him through fifteen years of dangerous missions.

"That's impossible," Elena said, but her voice lacked conviction.

"Is it? Think about it, Elena. The timing, the circumstances, the way your mother disappeared from her old life around the time you were born." Phoenix's voice was gentle but relentless. "Did she ever tell you anything about your father?"

"She said he was a good man who worked for the government, but that his job was too dangerous for them to be together." Elena's voice was barely above a whisper. "She said he never knew about me, that she made the choice to raise me alone to protect both of us."

The pieces were falling into place with devastating clarity. Maria had been pregnant with Phoenix's child when she'd disappeared from his life, choosing to raise their daughter in secret rather than expose her to the dangers of his world. Elena wasn't just Viktor's adopted daughter seeking revenge for her brother's death – she was Phoenix's biological daughter, manipulated by the man who had raised her into seeking vengeance against her own father.

"Oh God," Tori whispered, understanding the implications even before Phoenix could fully process them himself.

Elena was staring at Phoenix with a mixture of horror and recognition, seeing her own features reflected in his face. "You're my father," she said, the words coming out like an accusation.

"I think I am," Phoenix replied, his voice heavy with the weight of twenty-eight years of missed opportunities and unknown connections.

"This changes everything," Elena said, her carefully constructed plans crumbling around her.

"No," Phoenix said firmly. "It changes nothing about

what we need to do. Viktor is still a threat, his organization still needs to be stopped, and you still need to choose between the path of violence and the path of healing."

"But you're my father! I've spent eight years planning to kill my own father!"

"You've spent eight years being manipulated by a man who used your grief and your need for family to turn you into a weapon against the people who threatened his criminal empire." Phoenix's voice was steady, but Tori could see the pain in his eyes. "Viktor knew, Elena. He had to have known who your real father was when he took you in after Maria died."

The revelation hit Elena like a physical blow. She sank into one of the cabin's chairs, her face pale with shock and understanding.

"He knew," she whispered. "All this time, he knew, and he let me plan to kill you anyway."

"He used you," Phoenix said. "Just like he used Alexei. The only difference is that this time, he was using your love for your brother and your need to belong somewhere to manipulate you into destroying your own family."

Elena looked up at him, and Phoenix could see the war being fought behind her eyes. Everything she thought she knew about her life, her family, her purpose, had been called into question in the space of a few minutes.

"What do we do now?" she asked.

"Now we finish what we started," Phoenix replied. "We fake my death, we infiltrate Viktor's organization, and we bring it down from the inside. But we do it as a family, not as enemies."

"I don't know how to be your daughter," Elena said, her voice breaking.

"And I don't know how to be your father," Phoenix replied. "But we can learn together, after we make sure Viktor can never hurt anyone else's family the way he's hurt ours."

Tori watched the exchange with tears in her eyes, seeing the beginning of a healing that would take years to complete. Her husband had just discovered he had a daughter, and that daughter had just learned she'd been manipulated into trying to kill her own father. It was the kind of revelation that could destroy people or make them stronger, depending on how they chose to handle it.

"We need to move," Sarah's voice crackled through the earpiece. "Viktor's people are getting restless, and we're running out of time to stage this convincingly."

Phoenix looked at Elena, seeing his own determination reflected in her eyes. "Are you ready to help me die so that we can both live?"

Elena nodded, wiping away tears that were equal parts grief and hope. "Let's bring down Viktor Kozlov once and for all."

As they prepared for the final phase of their deception, Phoenix couldn't help but think about the strange turns that life could take. He'd come to this cabin expecting to die for the woman he loved, and instead he'd discovered a daughter he'd never known existed. The game was changing again, but this time, he had more to fight for than ever before.

The real battle was just beginning.

Chapter 12: Uncomfortable Truths

The silence in the cabin was deafening as the full

implications of the revelation settled over everyone present. Elena sat motionless in her chair, staring at Phoenix with eyes that held twenty-eight years of questions and a lifetime of missed connections. Tori watched her husband process the fact that he was a father, that the woman who had kidnapped her was his own daughter.

"I need to know everything," Elena said finally, her voice hollow. "About my mother, about you, about why she never told you about me."

Phoenix sat down across from her, and Tori could see him struggling to find the right words. "Maria was brilliant," he began. "She spoke seven languages fluently and had an intuitive understanding of cultural nuances that made her invaluable for intelligence work. We met during a joint operation in South America in 1994."

"What kind of operation?"

"Counter-narcotics. We were tracking a cocaine trafficking network that was using diplomatic pouches to smuggle drugs into the United States." Phoenix's voice was distant, remembering. "Maria was our cultural liaison, helping us understand the local power structures and navigate the political complexities."

Elena leaned forward, hungry for details about the mother she'd lost and the father she'd never known. "What was she like?"

"She was fearless but not reckless. Compassionate but not naive. She could see through people's lies and motivations, but she never became cynical about human nature." Phoenix smiled slightly. "She had this laugh that could light up an entire room, and she made the best coffee I've ever tasted."

"She still made amazing coffee when I was growing up," Elena said softly. "It was one of her few indulgences."

"We were together for about three months, during the operation and for a few weeks afterward. It was intense, the way relationships can be when you're living on adrenaline and shared danger." Phoenix's expression grew more serious. "But then I got called away for a long-term assignment in Eastern Europe. Deep cover work that would keep me out of contact for at least a year."

"And she never told you she was pregnant?"
"She never had the chance. By the time I got back to the States, she'd disappeared. No forwarding address, no contact information, no trace of where she'd gone."

Phoenix looked directly at Elena. "I tried to find her, but Maria was good at disappearing when she wanted to. It was part of what made her so effective in intelligence work."

Elena was quiet for a long moment, processing this information. "She told me that she left because your work was too dangerous, that she didn't want to raise a child in that world."

"She was right. The life I was living then wasn't compatible with family, with stability, with the kind of normal childhood that every kid deserves." Phoenix's voice carried the weight of regret. "If I'd known about you, I would have made different choices. But maybe Maria knew that, and maybe she thought those choices would have gotten all of us killed."

"So she went to Viktor instead?"

"Apparently. Though I'm still trying to understand how that connection developed." Phoenix frowned, thinking through the timeline. "Viktor's organization was already established by the mid-1990s, but he wasn't on our radar yet. It's possible that Maria encountered him through her translation work, or through other intelligence contacts."

Elena's expression darkened. "Viktor told me that my mother came to him for protection, that she was being hunted by American intelligence agencies who wanted to silence her."

"That's a lie. Maria was never a target, never in danger from her own government. If anything, she was one of our most trusted assets." Phoenix's voice was firm. "Viktor manipulated her just like he manipulated you, Elena. He used her fear and vulnerability to bring her into his organization."

"But why? What did he gain by taking in a pregnant translator and her child?"

"Long-term investment. Viktor was always thinking decades ahead, always looking for ways to gain leverage over his enemies." Phoenix's expression was grim. "He probably realized who your father was, and he saw an opportunity to create a weapon that could be used against me someday."

The words hit Elena like a physical blow. "You're saying he planned this from the beginning? That he raised me specifically to use against you?"

"I'm saying Viktor Kozlov is a master manipulator who never does anything without multiple layers of purpose. Taking in Maria and her child gave him a valuable translator, a potential intelligence asset, and a future weapon against one of his enemies." Phoenix's voice was gentle but relentless. "He's been playing a game that started before you were born, Elena."

Tori watched the exchange with growing understanding of the complexity of the situation they were facing. Viktor hadn't just been seeking revenge for his son's death – he'd been orchestrating a multi-generational campaign of manipulation and control that had turned a father and daughter into enemies.

"There's something else," Elena said, her voice barely above a whisper. "Something Viktor told me about the Prague operation that doesn't match what you've said."

"What?"

"He said that Alexei wasn't just a translator. He said that Alexei was working undercover for American intelligence, that he was feeding information to the CIA about Viktor's operations."

Phoenix felt the ground shift beneath him. If Alexei had been an intelligence asset, if he'd been working for the CIA, then his death in Prague took on an entirely different meaning.

"That's impossible," Phoenix said, but even as he spoke, he could hear the uncertainty in his own voice.

"Is it? Think about it. A nineteen-year-old college student who speaks six languages, who has access to his father's criminal organization, who needs money for medical school." Elena's voice was gaining strength. "Wouldn't that be exactly the kind of person the CIA would try to recruit?"

Phoenix's mind raced through the implications. If Alexei had been a CIA asset, then the Prague operation had been compromised from the beginning. Viktor would have known they were coming, would have had time to prepare, would have been able to manipulate the situation to his advantage.

"Sarah," Phoenix said, touching his earpiece. "I need you to run a check on Alexei Kozlov. See if he was ever recruited as an intelligence asset."
"Already on it," Sarah replied. "I started digging as soon as Elena mentioned the Prague discrepancies. Give me a few minutes to access the classified databases."

Elena watched Phoenix's face, seeing the doubt and

confusion that her revelation had created. "If Alexei was working for the CIA, then his death wasn't an accident, was it? It was an execution."

"No. Even if Alexei was an asset, even if he was feeding us information, that doesn't change what happened in that warehouse. He ran, my team member made a split second decision, and a young man died." Phoenix's voice was firm. "It was still a tragedy, Elena. It was still a mistake."

"But it was a mistake that Viktor could have prevented. If he knew Alexei was working for the CIA, if he knew the raid was coming, then he could have kept his son away from the warehouse that night."

The implication was staggering. Viktor might have deliberately put his own son in danger, knowing that the boy's death would provide the perfect justification for a campaign of revenge against the CIA operatives who had destroyed his organization.

"You're suggesting that Viktor sacrificed his own son to create a martyr?"

"I'm suggesting that Viktor Kozlov is capable of anything if it serves his long-term interests. Including the sacrifice of his own family." Elena's voice was bitter.

"He raised me to be a weapon against you, Marcus. Do you really think he wouldn't sacrifice Alexei to create the perfect motivation for that weapon?"

Sarah's voice crackled through the earpiece: "Phoenix, I've got the information you requested. Alexei Kozlov was indeed recruited as a CIA asset in early 1999, about six months before the Prague operation. He was providing intelligence about his father's weapons trafficking network."

The confirmation hit Phoenix like a hammer blow. Everything he thought he knew about Prague, about Alexei's death, about Viktor's motivations, had been called into question.

"There's more," Sarah continued. "According to the classified files, Alexei was supposed to be extracted before the raid. He was never supposed to be in that warehouse when the operation went down."

"Then why was he there?" Phoenix asked.
"Because someone told him to be there. Someone who knew about the operation and wanted him to be in the line of fire when it happened."

Elena closed her eyes, the final pieces of the puzzle falling into place. "Viktor knew. He knew about the raid, he knew about Alexei's CIA connection, and he made sure his son was in that warehouse when your team arrived."

"He sacrificed his own son to create the perfect revenge scenario," Phoenix said, the full scope of Viktor's manipulation finally becoming clear. "Alexei's death wasn't collateral damage – it was the opening move in a game that Viktor has been playing for eight years."

Tori felt sick as she processed the implications. Viktor had orchestrated his own son's death, raised Elena to be a weapon against her biological father, and manipulated everyone involved into a cycle of violence and revenge that served only his own twisted purposes.

"We have to stop him," Elena said, her voice carrying a new kind of determination. "Not just for Alexei, not just for us, but for everyone else he's manipulated and destroyed over the years."

"We will," Phoenix replied. "But first, we need to complete the deception. Viktor is expecting confirmation that I'm dead, and if we don't give it to him, he'll send backup that will compromise everything we're trying to accomplish."

Elena nodded, wiping away tears that were equal parts grief and rage. "What do you need me to do?"

"I need you to be the daughter Viktor raised you to be, just long enough to get close enough to destroy him." Phoenix's voice was steady, but Tori could see the pain in his eyes. "I need you to pretend that you succeeded in killing your father."

"And then?"

"Then we bring down his entire organization and make sure he can never manipulate another family the way he's manipulated ours."

As they prepared for the final phase of their deception, Phoenix couldn't help but think about the cruel ironies of the situation. He'd spent eight years carrying the guilt of Alexei's death, never knowing that the young man had been sacrificed by his own father. He'd built a new life as Marcus Sterling, never knowing that his own daughter was being raised to destroy him.

But now, with the truth finally revealed, they had a chance to end Viktor's reign of manipulation and violence once and for all. It would require them to trust each other completely, to work together despite the years of deception and pain that lay between them.

The game was entering its final phase, and this time, Phoenix intended to win not just for himself and Tori, but for the daughter he'd never known he had and the son Viktor had sacrificed for his own twisted purposes.

The reckoning was coming, and Viktor Kozlov was about to learn that some games had consequences he'd never anticipated.

Chapter 13: Into the Shadows

The staged death of Phoenix required a level of detail that would have impressed even the most paranoid intelligence operative. Sarah had coordinated with contacts in the medical examiner's office, the local police department, and even the regional news media to create a comprehensive fiction that would satisfy Viktor's need for verification.

"The official story is that you were killed during a shootout with Elena's team," Sarah explained as they reviewed the fabricated evidence. "Elena will report that you fought back, that there were casualties on both sides, but that she ultimately succeeded in completing the mission."

Phoenix studied the fake crime scene photos, seeing his own "corpse" lying in a pool of synthetic blood. The body was actually one of Elena's associates, a man of similar build who had volunteered to play dead in exchange for a new identity and safe passage out of Viktor's organization.

"What about dental records, fingerprints, DNA evidence?" Phoenix asked.

"All taken care of. The body will be too damaged by 'gunfire' for easy identification, and the official records will show that Marcus Sterling died in the mountains while trying to rescue his wife." Sarah's smile was grim. "As far as the world is concerned, you'll be a tragic victim of international terrorism."

Tori watched the preparations with a mixture of fascination and horror. Her husband was planning his own fake death with the same methodical precision he brought to his construction projects, treating it like just another problem to be solved through careful planning and execution.

"What about me?" she asked. "What's my story going to be?"

"You're the traumatized widow who witnessed her husband's murder and barely escaped with her life," Phoenix replied. "Elena will report that she let you go as a message to other former CIA operatives – that their families aren't safe, that Viktor's reach extends everywhere."

"And then what? I just disappear too?"

"You become Sarah Sterling, Marcus's grieving sister who takes you in during your time of loss." Phoenix's voice was gentle. "It's not a perfect cover, but it will hold up long enough for us to complete the mission against Viktor."

Elena had been quiet during most of the planning, but now she spoke up. "There's something else we need to consider. Viktor will want to meet with me personally after this operation. He'll want to debrief me, to hear the details firsthand, to make sure I'm ready for the next phase of his revenge campaign."

"Which gives us the opportunity we need to get close to him," Phoenix said.

"It also puts me in incredible danger. If Viktor suspects that I've betrayed him, if he realizes that you're still alive, he'll kill me slowly and painfully." Elena's voice was steady, but Phoenix could see the fear in her eyes.

"We won't let that happen."

"How can you be sure? You don't know Viktor the way I do. You don't understand how paranoid he is, how many layers of security he maintains around himself."

Phoenix looked at his daughter — the word still felt strange in his mind — and saw himself reflected in her determination and her fear. "Because we're going to give him exactly what he wants to see. A grieving daughter who has finally avenged her brother's death, who is ready to take her place in his organization as his heir and successor."

"And if he doesn't believe the performance?"
"Then we improvise. But Elena, you need to understand something. This isn't just about bringing down Viktor's organization anymore. This is about saving you from the life he's trapped you in, about giving you the chance to choose your own path."

Elena stared at him, and Phoenix could see the conflict in her eyes. Part of her wanted to believe that redemption was possible, that she could escape the cycle of violence that had defined her entire existence.

But another part of her was terrified of trusting anyone, especially the man she'd been raised to hate.

"I don't know how to be anything other than what Viktor made me," she said quietly.

"You'll learn. We'll learn together." Phoenix's voice was firm. "But first, we have to survive the next few days."

The plan they developed was complex and dangerous, requiring precise timing and flawless execution. Elena would return to Viktor with evidence of Phoenix's death, allowing herself to be debriefed and celebrated as the daughter who had finally avenged her brother. Meanwhile, Phoenix and Tori would disappear into new identities, working with Sarah to gather intelligence about Viktor's organization and plan their final assault.

"The key is patience," Sarah explained as they prepared to separate. "Viktor will be euphoric about Phoenix's death, but he'll also be planning his next moves. We need to let him reveal his full network before we strike."

"How long are we talking about?" Phoenix asked.

"Weeks, maybe months. Viktor has been building this

organization for decades, and he won't expose all of his assets and operations immediately." Sarah's expression was serious. "This is a long-term operation, not a quick strike."

Phoenix looked at Tori, seeing the strain that the past few days had put on her. She'd been kidnapped, learned that her husband was a former CIA operative, discovered that her kidnapper was his daughter, and now she was being asked to fake her own death and disappear into a new identity.

"Are you okay with this?" he asked her.

"I'm okay with whatever it takes to keep us safe and bring Viktor to justice," Tori replied. "But Marcus, I need you to promise me something."

"What?"
"Promise me that when this is over, when Viktor is stopped and Elena is safe, we'll find a way to build a real life together. Not Marcus Sterling the fake identity, not Phoenix the CIA operative, but the real you, whoever that is."

Phoenix took her hands in his, feeling the weight of everything they'd been through and everything that lay ahead. "I promise. When this is over, we'll figure out who we really are, together."

As the sun set over the Cascade Mountains, they put their plan into motion. Elena and her remaining associate loaded the fake body into their vehicle, along with the fabricated evidence that would convince Viktor of Phoenix's death. Phoenix and Tori prepared to disappear into the network of safe houses and false identities that Sarah had established over the years.

"Remember," Phoenix said to Elena as they prepared to part ways, "you're not just acting a role. You're infiltrating Viktor's organization to destroy it from within. Trust your instincts, but don't take unnecessary risks."

"What if something goes wrong? What if Viktor suspects the deception?"

"Then you run. You disappear, and you let us handle Viktor through other means." Phoenix's voice was firm. "Your safety is more important than the mission, Elena. Don't ever forget that."

Elena nodded, but Phoenix could see the doubt in her eyes. She'd been raised in Viktor's world, where loyalty was everything and betrayal was punished by death. The idea of putting her own safety above the mission went against everything she'd been taught.

"I'll be in contact through secure channels," Sarah said, handing Elena a small communication device. "Check in every forty-eight hours, but be careful. Viktor's people are sophisticated, and they'll be monitoring for any signs of deception."

As Elena drove away into the darkness, Phoenix felt a mixture of pride and terror. His daughter was walking back into the lion's den, carrying with her the hopes of everyone Viktor had ever manipulated or destroyed. If she succeeded, they would have the intelligence they needed to bring down one of the world's most dangerous criminal organizations. If she failed, she would die, and Viktor would know that Phoenix was still alive.

"She's brave," Tori said, watching the taillights disappear into the forest.
"She's terrified," Phoenix replied. "But she's doing it anyway, which is what real courage looks like."

They climbed into Sarah's extraction vehicle, a nondescript SUV that would take them to the first of several safe houses. As they drove through the mountains, Phoenix found himself thinking about the strange turns that life could take. Twenty-four hours ago, he'd been a successful real estate developer with a loving wife and a carefully constructed normal life. Now he was a dead man, traveling with his grieving "widow" and planning the destruction of a criminal empire run by the man who had raised his daughter to kill him.

"What are you thinking about?" Tori asked.

"Family. How it can be the most important thing in the world and the most dangerous thing in the world, sometimes at the same time."

"Elena will be okay. She's stronger than she knows, and she has something Viktor never gave her – a reason to hope for something better."

Phoenix squeezed Tori's hand, drawing strength from her certainty. She was right, of course. Elena did have something that Viktor's manipulation couldn't destroy – the possibility of redemption, of choosing a different path, of building a life based on love instead of hatred.

But first, they had to survive the game that Viktor had been playing for eight years. And that game was about to enter its most dangerous phase.

Meanwhile, Elena was driving through the night toward

a meeting that would determine the fate of everyone she'd come to care about. In the back of her vehicle, the fake evidence of Phoenix's death would either convince Viktor that his long-sought revenge was complete, or it would expose the deception and doom them all.

The next few hours would determine whether the Kozlov family's reign of manipulation and violence would finally come to an end, or whether it would claim even more victims in its relentless pursuit of power and revenge.

As Elena approached Viktor's compound, she took a deep breath and prepared to give the performance of her life. Everything depended on her ability to convince the man who had raised her that she had successfully killed her own father.

The final act was about to begin.

Chapter 14: The Puppet Master

Viktor Kozlov's compound sat on fifty acres of heavily forested land in the mountains of British Columbia, a fortress disguised as a luxury retreat. From the air, it looked like the kind of place where wealthy executives might hold corporate retreats or where celebrities might escape from the pressures of public life. But Elena knew better. She knew about the underground bunkers, the sophisticated security systems, the armed guards who patrolled the perimeter with military precision.

As her vehicle approached the main gate, Elena forced herself to breathe slowly and evenly. Everything depended on her ability to convince Viktor that she had succeeded in killing Phoenix, that his long-sought revenge was finally complete. One wrong word, one suspicious gesture, and she would join the long list of people who had underestimated Viktor Kozlov's paranoia.

The guards at the gate recognized her immediately, waving her through with the kind of deference reserved for family members. Elena had grown up on this compound, had learned to shoot and fight and think tactically within these walls. It had been her home, her prison, and her training ground all at once.

Viktor was waiting for her in his study, a room that managed to be both elegant and intimidating. The walls were lined with books in a dozen languages, and the furniture was expensive but understated. It was the office of a man who wielded enormous power but preferred to do so from the shadows.

"Elena," Viktor said, rising from behind his desk with a smile that didn't reach his eyes. "My dear daughter. Tell me everything."

Elena had rehearsed this moment during the long drive from the mountains, but now, faced with the man who had raised her and manipulated her for twenty-eight years, she felt the weight of the deception she was attempting.

"It's done," she said simply, setting a briefcase on Viktor's desk. "Phoenix is dead."

Viktor's smile widened, and for a moment, Elena could see genuine joy in his expression. "Show me."

Elena opened the briefcase, revealing the fabricated evidence that Sarah had prepared. Crime scene photographs, medical examiner's preliminary report, even a recording of the supposed gunfight that had led to Phoenix's death. Viktor examined each piece of evidence with the careful attention of someone who had survived decades in a world where deception was commonplace.

"The body was badly damaged," Elena explained. "But

the dental records match, and the DNA analysis is being expedited through our contacts in the medical examiner's office."

"And the wife? Tori Sterling?"

"I let her go, as we discussed. She'll spread the word about what happened, about how easily we reached Phoenix despite all his precautions." Elena kept her voice steady, professional. "She's traumatized, broken. She won't be a threat to our operations."

Viktor nodded approvingly. "Good. Fear is often more effective than death when it comes to sending messages." He set down the photographs and looked at Elena directly. "How do you feel, my dear? You've finally avenged your brother's death. You've completed the mission that has defined your entire adult life."

Elena had prepared for this question, but it was still difficult to answer convincingly. "I feel... empty. I thought killing Phoenix would bring me peace, would somehow bring Alexei back. But it doesn't change anything. My brother is still dead."

"Ah, but that's where you're wrong." Viktor moved around his desk to stand beside Elena, placing a paternal hand on her shoulder. "Alexei's death wasn't meaningless if it led to this moment. His sacrifice gave us the motivation we needed to strike back at our enemies, to show them that the Kozlov family doesn't forget and doesn't forgive."

The words made Elena's skin crawl, but she forced herself to nod in agreement. "What happens now?"

"Now we move to the next phase of our campaign. Phoenix was just the beginning, Elena. There are fourteen other former CIA operatives who were involved in the Prague operation, and they all need to pay for what they did to our family."

Elena felt a chill run down her spine. Viktor wasn't satisfied with Phoenix's supposed death – he was planning a systematic campaign of revenge that would target dozens of innocent people.

"Fourteen others?"

www.ingramcontent.com/pod-product-compliance
Lightning Source LLC
Chambersburg PA
CBHW060648260626
47161CB00008B/3044